THE NEW KID IN TOWN . . .

"Meeting you was the best thing that's happened to me since I came to town," Jay told her.

"I was probably just the first person you saw," Anne teased.

"That's not true. I spent all morning down at the store."

"The store?"

He nodded. "Ogden's," he said.

Suddenly it hit her. She knew the Ogden son was in town to look over the store, but Anne hadn't expected him to be a boy her age.

"You never told me your last name," she said, hoping.

"And you didn't tell me yours."

"Hollis," she said, waiting for his reaction.

"Hollis." He hesitated. "Isn't that the name of . . ."

"That's right. David Hollis, the manager of Ogden's, is my father. He's the man you've been sent to check on . . ."

The Latest Books from SIGNET VISTA

ANNE
and
JAY

BARBARA BARTHOLOMEW

A SIGNET VISTA BOOK
NEW AMERICAN LIBRARY
TIMES MIRROR

NAL BOOKS ARE AVAILABLE AT QUANTITY DISCOUNTS
WHEN USED TO PROMOTE PRODUCTS OR SERVICES. FOR
INFORMATION PLEASE WRITE TO PREMIUM MARKETING DIVISION,
THE NEW AMERICAN LIBRARY, INC., 1633 BROADWAY,
NEW YORK, NEW YORK 10019.

RL 6/IL 6+

SIGNET VISTA TRADEMARK REG. U.S. PAT. OFF. AND FOREIGN COUNTRIES
REGISTERED TRADEMARK—MARCA REGISTRADA
HECHO EN CHICAGO, IL., U.S.A.

SIGNET, SIGNET CLASSICS, MENTOR, PLUME, MERIDIAN AND NAL
BOOKS are published by The New American Library, Inc.,
1633 Broadway, New York, New York 10019

First Printing, July, 1982

1   2   3   4   5   6   7   8   9

PRINTED IN THE UNITED STATES OF AMERICA

To the Ericksons

1

Anne broke into a run as she hurried toward her after-school job at Ogden's department store. It made no difference that she was the boss's daughter; Mrs. Turner would have her head if she was five minutes late!

Dad was out of town anyway. A sense of adventure glowed somewhere in Anne's midsection as she reminded herself that both Mom and Dad would be away for two whole weeks. It wasn't that she wouldn't miss them, but it was exciting to know she and her sisters were in charge of things at home all by themselves for those two weeks. It was such a glorious feeling of freedom.

No need to start off this first day by being yelled at by her supervisor. Anne slowed her pace as she entered the store, walking sedately past the few customers shopping at this time of day.

She smiled at co-workers as she went by. "Hi, Roger," she called. "Mrs. Wattley. Hi, Chad."

She kept the smile carefully plastered on her face as she approached junior sportswear, the spot in the store where she worked each afternoon after school. It wasn't always easy to smile at Mrs. Turner.

"Good afternoon, Anne." The immaculate Mrs. Turner greeted her with a chilly air, reaching up to smooth carefully colored blond hair with a slender hand tipped with vivid nail polish. Anne always thought Mrs. Turner looked more like one of the plastic dummies used to model clothes in Ogden's than a real person. She was lovely to look at, but stiff and cold. "I'm so glad you condescended to drop in."

Anne tried to smother a sigh. Sometimes being the boss's daughter made things twice as hard. "I'm right on time," she said, carefully polite. She pointed to the clock on the wall at the back of the store just behind the shoe department. "And I had to hurry because Mrs. Markham kept me after class. She wanted to know why I couldn't make the kind of grades Nikki did when she was in algebra."

"Nicole is an excellent student." Mrs. Turner's tone was reproving. "You could profit by your sister's example."

Anne felt her face burn. If there was one thing she hated, it was being compared to either of her sisters. Nikki and Leslie were okay, she supposed, but anyone who'd lived in the same house with them the way Anne had all of her fifteen years, would know they were a long way from perfect.

"Your other sister is outstanding as well." Mrs. Turner wasn't through.

Anne was tired of this. Pointedly she began work on the display of new fall shirts. "Nobody has ever accused Leslie of being a super student."

"But so lovely and talented." Mrs. Turner's voice was suddenly sweet as whipped cream. "Your parents must be so proud to have a daughter like her . . . cheerleader, student-council president, and so popular . . . I'm sure the boys simply flock to her."

"They flock all over the place," Anne admitted reluctantly, rebuttoning a peppy plaid shirt that a customer had left in disarray. She wondered why it was that sour-tempered Mrs. Turner could approve of both her sisters, but not of her.

"Goodness, what are we doing standing around chatting?" Mrs. Turner spoke as though it was all Anne's fault. "And today of all days!"

Anne moved slowly through the department, straightening and arranging. She felt a particular responsibility to do her part to keep the store looking good while Dad was out of town and had to leave its management to his assistant. "What's so important about today?" she asked, only half-interested.

"You haven't heard?" Mrs. Turner trailed after her, the

spark in her eyes indicating she was about to impart a select morsel of gossip.

"I guess not." Anne was hardly interested. In the back of her mind she was already planning how she would spend this evening and all the others in the two weeks Mom and Dad would be gone. It wasn't that she planned to lead a wild and dissolute life. There was little-enough oportunity for that sort of thing in a small town like Bryan, but it would be great to make her own decisions, to choose for herself what she would eat and when she would go to bed. She was really looking forward to it.

Mrs. Turner stepped conspiratorially closer, leaning over to whisper in Anne's face. A drift of heavily scented perfume reached Anne, making her eyes water.

"We have an important visitor," Mrs. Turner whispered.

Anne shrugged. She couldn't imagine anyone important visiting Bryan. "Who is it?" she asked indifferently. She could just imagine the kind of person Mrs. Turner would think important.

"It's the Ogden son." The whisper was only slightly louder. "And you can guess why he's here."

Anne's interest picked up slightly. She had never met a member of the family who owned the small chain of department stores for which both her parents worked, Mom as bookkeeper and Dad as store manager. Normally the division manager served as the link with the headquarters and this store.

"What's he doing here when Dad's out of town?" she asked, frowning. It didn't make sense. After all these years—years when most of the time she thought of the store as truly her father's—why had the real owner, or his son, shown up?

"You can surely guess," Mrs. Turner said again, her voice malicious.

Anne's busy hands stopped their work. "What do you mean?" she asked.

Mrs. Turner looked around the store. "What does it usually mean when someone that high up comes to take a look at a store? Someone at the top wants to know what's going on."

"But everything's fine here," Anne countered angrily. Was Mrs. Turner implying that Dad wasn't the best manager the chain had?

"Apparently not everyone thinks so," Mrs. Turner answered smugly.

A customer entered the department at that moment and Anne had to plaster her smile back on and attend to business, but the nagging problem presented by Mrs. Turner's words hovered unpleasantly at the back of her mind. That first customer was followed by a steady stream of others and Anne had little time to consider the matter. But it gave her a sick feeling to think the company for which Dad had worked so long was taking advantage of his absence to snoop.

It was a little after six when she finally got off work, having helped an elderly woman make up her mind about a gift for a granddaughter, and she was tired from the long day at school and at work.

As she left the store she tried to push the possibility of problems there to the back of her mind. She'd looked forward to these two weeks, the first time Dad and Mom had gone away without insisting Gran come and stay with the girls. But even Mom had been forced to admit that with Nikki starting college in a few days and Leslie already a senior at the high school, they were surely old enough to look after themselves.

"But I'll never admit my baby is grown up," she'd added with misty eyes, patting Anne's shoulder.

Baby! Anne was indignant again at the thought. Here she was beginning her sophomore year at high school, and just because she was the youngest, the whole family still thought of her as the baby. It wasn't fair! She'd show them she could be as grown-up as Nikki or Leslie.

Anne walked slowly from the downtown area, past the college, moving steadily along tree-lined streets to her own home. The routine of school and work was familiar to her, but somehow she was extra tired today. She was glad it was Nikki's turn to make dinner.

Perhaps it was the thought of trouble at the store. Dad and Mom had gone off so happily to California, like two little kids freed from school for the first time in ages. She didn't want them to come back to problems.

Anne shook her head. It was silly to borrow trouble over something Mrs. Turner said. Mrs. Turner liked to imagine problems, particularly for other people.

She relaxed and tried to enjoy her walk. It was early September and fall hadn't yet begun to poke its face into the setting. Summer was at its most lush moment and Anne sniffed at the sweet scent of late roses in a neighbor's garden. The last block before home was always the hardest to climb, for the little town sprawled on gentle hills and the neighborhood where the Hollis family lived was on one of the highest of them.

Honk!

Anne jumped about a foot into the air at the sudden sound of a car horn from behind her. She turned angrily. Who could be honking and scaring her to death that way?

Her anger increased when she saw the little red sports car and the stranger climbing from behind its wheel.

"Sorry," a tall, red-haired boy apologized sheepishly. "I was getting out of my car and accidentally hit the horn with my elbow. Hope I didn't startle you."

His grin was disarming. "Not too much," Anne admitted cautiously. She hoped she hadn't looked like an idiot leaping into the air that way.

Then she noticed the small suitcase he pulled from the car.

"Are you visiting the Harrisons?" she asked, nodding toward the nearest house.

He looked toward it. "The Harrisons?" he asked, sounding confused.

"They live in that house," Anne explained. "I thought you might be a friend or a relative or something. Now that school has started we won't see many visitors in Bryan, most people come during the summer."

Darn! There she went again, chattering away like a magpie out of nervousness. Why was it so difficult to meet a new boy, particularly an attractive one like this? She drew a deep breath and hoped he was looking at her that way because he thought she was interesting—and not because she was acting strangely.

She tried to think how Leslie would have handled this situation . . . but then, Leslie had an advantage, she was so pretty that it was the boys who got nervous and said all the wrong things.

"I *am* visiting," he explained, "that is, I don't live here, I'm just here temporarily, but I don't know anyone named Harrison. Isn't this 522 Mulberry?"

Anne shook her head. "This is Canterbury Lane," she said. "Mulberry is across town, though in a town this size that isn't so very far."

"Oh." He looked at the big two-story frame house with a regretful air. "For such a small town, it sure is hard finding your way around here."

Anne laughed, forgetting her own discomfort in considering his problems. "I'll direct you," she offered. "Just go past the supermarket to Ryerson's, then turn—"

"Ryerson's?" he questioned.

"The drugstore. It's ages old and they still have an old-fashioned soda fountain where you can get things like cherry phosphates, though the chocolate shakes are my favorite."

"I see," he said, sounding as though he didn't see at all.

"From Ryerson's you go on down Main until you get to Ogden's—"

"That's the department store." He nodded, understanding.

Anne smiled, pleased he at least knew the name of the store her father managed. Ogden's might not be a large chain, but its name was recognized throughout the state. "Just past Ogden's parking lot, you turn south. It's only about six blocks straight south, then you turn east . . . though the road squiggles a little so you have to be sure not to miss the turnoff."

By now the red-haired boy was looking thoroughly confused. "Do you think you could show me the way?" he asked.

Anne looked at the red Corvette. She wouldn't mind taking a ride in it, particularly not if some of her friends should happen to see her. "Mom would have a fit if she heard I went riding around town with a stranger."

His slow smile spread to his greenish eyes. He stuck out a hand. "I'm Jay."

"I'm Anne." She matched his smile. Most boys were hard to talk to, but somehow this one wasn't. Surely Mom would understand that she was simply being a good Samaritan, offering this newcomer a helping hand.

She hesitated.

"How about it, Anne?" he asked. "Will you be my guide?"

She nodded. He walked around to open the car door for her. Boys never opened doors for Anne, though they frequently did for Leslie. The guys practically stood in line to do things for Leslie.

Anne enjoyed the feel of the powerful little car as it moved effortlessly down shady streets. Out of the corner of her eye, she kept a lookout for acquaintances. It was nearly impossible to walk a single block in Bryan without seeing someone you knew, but this afternoon everyone seemed to have vanished—probably because it was dinnertime.

"Looking for someone?" Jay asked.

"No." Anne tried not to look embarrassed. It was easy enough to guide him now that she was sitting right in the car beside him. They went past Ryerson's, past Ogden's, then turned south. Jay stopped his car in front of the comfortable rooming house at 522 Mulberry.

"Thanks to you, I've finally found it." He turned to her.

Anne shrugged, disclaiming credit. "You'll be staying here, then?"

"For a couple of weeks anyway. My dad made arrangements for me."

"There're some new motels out on the highway outside of town," Anne told him. From the Corvette, she'd have expected him to be more the fancy-motel type.

"This place was recommended to my dad," he explained. "He thought it would be a better place for me to stay."

Anne nodded doubtfully. If she was ever lucky enough to get to go away from home by herself, she sure wouldn't

stay at a place like Mrs. Fumble's. She would choose
something more adventurous.

"Mrs. Fumble runs this place," she told him. "She's a
nice lady, I guess, but she runs everything—the PTA, the
church, almost the town. I have a feeling she'll be telling
you what time to go to bed and what to eat for breakfast."

The idea didn't seem to upset him. "Maybe that's what
Dad had in mind when he chose this place."

Anne shook her head. "If I was getting off on my own,
I sure wouldn't want somebody telling me what to do. I
get enough of that at home. My mom is an expert."

His look was suddenly serious. "My mother died when
I was little," he said, "and my dad is always so involved
with his business that I've always been kind of on my
own. There're times when I wouldn't mind having someone telling me what to do."

Anne stared. She hadn't known before how attractive
the ordinary combination of freckles and red hair could
be. She liked his clean, slightly outdoorsy scent. "If you
ever want to be bossed around, come over to my place.
We have a full staff, including my two older sisters."

"I might take you up on that." He looked at her as
though he too liked what he saw. Anne hoped fervently
he never saw Leslie. Nobody ever noticed her when the
blond bombshell was around.

Still, maybe he was too young for Leslie, who liked
them at least eighteen and preferably a little older than
that.

"How old are you?" she asked, then blushed at the
abruptness of the question.

"Sixteen," he answered, not seeming to find the question odd. "How about you?"

"I'm fifteen. I'm in the tenth grade at the high school. I
don't suppose you'll be going to school here if you're only
visiting?" She tried to keep the question from sounding
too wistful.

"Nothing's definite right now. Dad's still making
plans."

"And in the meantime you don't have to go to school?"

One eyebrow arched questioningly. "It's a very temporary situation," he told her. "If there's one thing Dad feels strongly about, it's education, high school and college. He's afraid I won't follow in his footsteps and be a super success if I don't go to school."

He sounded as though being a super success was not one of his own goals. Anne would have like to ask him about that, but decided she'd already asked too many questions. Besides, Nikki was most likely having a fit wondering where she was right now.

"I'd better get home," she said, starting to climb from the car.

He frowned. "Where do you think you're going?"

"I'm going to get out and walk home. My sisters will be expecting me."

He reached across to close the door she'd opened. "I'm not going to reward you for doing a favor for me by making you walk home." He started the car's engine. "I'll drive you."

She laughed as they moved down the street. "This could be a problem," she pointed out. "Once we get back in my neighborhood, do I have to show you the way back over here again?"

His deep laugh matched hers. "And then when we get back over here again, I'll need to drive you back home."

"Round and round we go." Anne settled back against the new-smelling leather of the upholstery. This was fun.

"Don't worry," Jay told her. "I paid attention as we drove over. I can find my way back next time."

Anne was almost regretful. The favor was over. He wouldn't need her next time.

They reached the downtown area and turned past Ogden's, but when they got to Ryerson's, he pulled into the parking lot. She looked up at him, puzzled.

"Didn't you tell me you like chocolate shakes?"

Briefly Anne thought about Nikki and Leslie and the dinner that was doubtless already prepared and cooling at home. Well, the whole point of this two weeks was to show how independent she was. How much on her own was she if she had to dance to the schedule her sisters had set up? She could make her own decisions!

"I'd love a chocolate shake," she agreed, hoping des-

perately that at least one or two of the high-school crowd
would be in Ryerson's, preferably someone talkative
enough to tell everyone else that Anne Hollis had been
seen in Ryerson's with an attractive boy who drove an ex-
pensive-looking Corvette.

She went ahead of him into the drugstore, savoring the
coolness of its air-conditioning as she stepped inside. The
calendar might say fall, but the weather was still lingering
in summer.

Disappointingly the place was empty except for old Mr.
Ryerson and the elderly woman he was waiting on back
in the pharmacy.

"Be with you in a minute, Anne," gray-haired Mr. Ryerson called.

"Tell me," Jay demanded as the two of them settled
into a booth. "Do you know everyone in town? You knew
my landlady and now you know the pharmacist."

"Everyone in Bryan knows practically everyone else,"
Anne explained, suddenly feeling almost shy. Abruptly
they didn't seem to have anything to say to each other,
and Anne started reading the menu with apparently avid
interest while Jay studied the ancient furnishings of the
soda fountain.

"I never saw a place like this before in my life," he
said.

"Mr. Ryerson keeps talking about updating and making everything all modern." Anne was glad for a topic
to talk about.

"That would be a shame. You can find modern all over
the place, but this is really something."

"That's the way I feel," Anne agreed.

When Mr. Ryerson came over to the booth, he frowned
at Jay. "What'll it be?" he asked Anne, ignoring her companion. Anne wished she'd thought to explain to Jay
about Mr. Ryerson's distrust of strangers.

"Jay and I both want chocolate shakes," she explained
hurriedly, then thought maybe she shouldn't have. Maybe
he'd changed his mind and wanted something different.
Maybe he hated chocolate shakes.

"That right?" Mr. Ryerson drawled, looking suspiciously at the boy, as though suspecting him of being a

blackmailer or bank robber or some other equally unworthy character. "This fellow your cousin from out of town or something, Anne?"

It was so embarrassing.

"No, Mr. Ryerson. Jay and I aren't related."

Mr. Ryerson bent closer to Jay, peering nearsightedly over half-sized glasses. "You new around here, son?"

"Yes, sir." Jay was suddenly stiff and formal and Anne couldn't blame him. Mr. Ryerson, who had known all three Hollis girls since they were babies, was acting like he was her father, though even Dad wouldn't be this embarrassing.

"We'd like our shakes, Mr. Ryerson. We're thirsty." It was bad enough when your own family treated you like a baby, Anne decided, but when the whole town thought it had a right to look after you . . . She could imagine herself at ninety with some descendant of Mr. Ryerson's inspecting her dates.

Dates! Not that this was the real thing. She hadn't gone on many real dates, hardly more than an outing with a whole bunch of kids, or maybe walking down to a movie with a guy she'd known since infancy.

But perhaps, after this, if Jay liked her enough and Mr. Ryerson didn't scare him off completely, maybe he'd say, "Anne, there's a super picture playing . . ." or "Anne, there's a little dance at school . . ." or "Anne. . . ."

"Anne!" Mr. Ryerson said her name as though he'd already said it several times without getting her attention. "I was just saying it's too close to dinnertime for you to be having a malted. How about a nice glass of iced tea to cool you off on a hot day?"

Anne looked at Jay. He shrugged. "Whatever you want," he told her.

All the fun had gone out of the outing. Now Jay knew she was treated like a baby who didn't know her own mind.

Deliberately Anne put on her most adult voice. "We'd prefer two chocolate shakes, Mr. Ryerson."

"I don't know what your mama would say." He walked back to the fountain, mumbling to himself. Anne watched

as he began to scoop ice cream into the tall metal con-
tainers in which he mixed his undeniably excellent shakes.

"He's terribly slow," Anne explained to Jay, "but nobody can make things like Mr. Ryerson. He tries to teach
the high-school kids who work for him how to do it, but
nobody else comes close."

"He's kind of different." Jay too was watching the
older man. It was as if neither of them dared look at the
other, but Jay sounded like himself again instead of all
stiff and phony formal, the way he had when Mr. Ryerson
was there. "I mean, telling a customer what to order. Nobody would do that back home."

"You must live in a city," Anne said with a sigh.

"I'm from Houston."

"It's my ambition to live in a city like that, where I
don't know a soul. As soon as I get out of school, the first
thing I'm going to do is move to the biggest one I can
find."

Mr. Ryerson was back, plopping thick chocolaty drinks
in front of them with an injured air. "Better hurry with
those," he ordered, "or that sister of yours will be getting
worried."

Anne stared at the tall glass, refusing to answer.
Naturally Mr. Ryerson knew Mom and Dad were out of
town. Everybody in town probably knew by now. There
were no secrets in Bryan.

"I'm looking after myself while my parents are away,
Mr. Ryerson."

His only answer was a disbelieving grunt, and Anne
was glad that he walked away without further comment.

Jay sipped at his shake. "This is good."

"I think so." Anne smiled at him, glad they shared the
same taste in drinks at least.

She sipped slowly at the shake, trying to make both it
and the moment last.

"So you want to move to the city," Jay commented
with an air of trying to get the conversation moving again.

Anne nodded. "I can't help envying you."

He looked around at the old drugstore. "I kind of like
what I see here." His eyes came back to rest on her face

and she wondered if he was talking about the store or about her. "I'm hoping Dad might decide to move here."

"Could that happen?" Anne forgot to be shy. "You really might move here?"

He lifted his eyebrows. "Depends on what happens while I'm here," he said.

She smiled at him. "I hope it works out."

He smiled back. "I do too . . . now."

Even the slowest-sipped shakes vanish eventually, and accompanied by warning glares from Mr. Ryerson, the two of them finally left the store and Jay drove her back up the hill toward home.

Anne got out of the car. "Sure you can find your way back?" she asked teasingly.

"I believe so." He grinned. "But maybe you'll show me around some more tomorrow if we get permission from Mr. Ryerson."

"Sure." Suddenly Anne felt as light as air. "I'd like that."

She watched as he drove away, then floated up the steps to the front porch. She had just put her foot on the first step when the front door was flung open.

A petite dark-haired girl with sparkling brown eyes regarded her angrily. "Who was that boy in the flashy sports car?" she demanded. "Where have you been? You should have been home to dinner an hour ago! What will Mom and Dad say?"

All the sparkling loveliness of the evening vanished like a bursting bubble. Anne drew in a deep breath. "I'm not a child," she said, and walked across the porch and past her sister into the house.

"Don't think you can ignore me, young lady," Nikki's voice followed her. "I'm in charge, with Mom and Dad away."

At the door to the kitchen, Anne was confronted by her other sister. Leslie was mad too, though her green eyes sparkled less brightly than Nikki's. Nikki's anger was like the sudden burst of a forest fire, but Leslie's smoldered like coals left in the fireplace.

"We were worried about you, Anne," she said. "You

could at least have had the courtesy to call and say you
were going to be late."

Once again, Anne took in a deep breath. Count to ten.
Control yourself. Don't let these two force you into a
scene.

"I'm on my own while Mom and Dad are gone." She
tried to use the most reasonable tone within her ability,
but somehow her voice trembled ever so slightly. "Neither
of you can tell me what to do."

"You're only a child," Leslie observed, smiling slightly.

But there was nothing humorous in Nikki's voice.
"We'll call Mom and Dad in California," she threatened.
"They'll tell you who's in charge."

2

The last thing Anne wanted was to see Mom and Dad's vacation spoiled by a call from home. She looked slowly around the up-to-date kitchen that Mom had had installed five years ago, saying that although she loved old houses, aging kitchens and bathrooms were quite another matter.

Very deliberately she walked over to the refrigerator, opened it, and took out the milk. She carried the container over to the cabinet and reached for a glass.

"What are you doing?" Nikki demanded, her small frame still all fire.

"Getting myself a glass of milk," Anne answered, pouring milk into the glass.

"Dinner was ready an hour ago," Leslie informed her icily. "If you were hungry, you should have come home then."

Anne studied her two sisters objectively. She didn't want to say she was too full of ice cream to be hungry, that getting the glass of milk was only something to do to keep from losing her temper, thus forcing Nikki into going through with her threat of calling their parents.

She knew her oldest sister well. Give Nikki about five minutes for the burst of temper to pass and she would be the most reasonable person in the world.

"Sorry if you were worried," she said, sitting down at the kitchen table.

"Sorry!" Nikki exploded. "Sorry! Both Leslie and I have plans for the evening and we've been stuck here wondering about you."

"I certainly didn't plan to spend the evening baby-sitting," Leslie agreed.

Baby-sitting! Anne felt her own temper flare. But she'd

15

had more experience keeping it under control than either of her sisters. When you were the youngest, when for years both of them were big enough to sit on you and make you do whatever they wanted, you learned the hard way to connive instead of fight.

Count to ten, Anne, she told herself. Mentally she began to count: One, two, three, four . . .

But Nikki's five-minute flare of temper was about up. Already the fire in her eyes was beginning to fade. "Look, Annie," she said, using the ancient nickname Anne had always hated. "We didn't mean to come on so strong and I won't call Mom and Dad this time—"

"You couldn't call them anyway," Leslie observed. "They're still on the road. Mom said they were going to take their time driving out."

Nikki ignored her middle sister. "The thing is that I'm responsible for you."

"*We're* responsible," Leslie added.

Nikki nodded without looking at Leslie. "Who was that boy, Anne? I didn't recognize the car."

"His name is Jay," Anne admitted reluctantly, feeling that the lovely afternoon was being spoiled by too much handling.

"Jay," Leslie mused. "I don't know anyone by that name."

No, Anne told herself, hoping her middle sister never set her lovely eyes on the red-haired boy, at least not until the two of them were already firmly acquainted.

"Who is he?" Nikki, though calm now, was not about to be swayed from the subject.

"Just a boy."

"I don't know many boys around here who drive Corvettes," Leslie commented. Both girls settled in chairs across from Anne. She felt like a prisoner being questioned. Anger began to rise in her once more.

"How did you meet him?" Nikki questioned.

"He stopped and asked for directions. He's staying at Mrs. Fumble's place."

"A teenage boy at a rooming house? What are his parents like? Just how old is he?"

Anne cast her gaze heavenward. Mom at her very

worst would never act like this. She was going to have to
risk a confrontation or else Nikki was going to sew up the
whole two weeks of freedom into something tighter than
usual.

"He's sixteen," she explained patiently. "And he's here
alone, so I haven't met his parents." Carefully she kept
her tone even as she added, "He's a nice boy I just met, a
friend, and I've told you all I'm going to. You're not responsible for me. I'm fifteen years old and I'm responsible
for myself."

She was surprised that the kitchen walls didn't fall
down as she stood up and, taking her full glass of milk
with her, marched out of the room.

"Anne, you come right back here," she heard Nikki
call after her, but she ignored the summons and went on
up to her room, closing and locking the door behind her.

She felt a sudden sense of release. It was independence
day. She had made her declaration, and when you came
right down to it, what could either Leslie or Nikki do?

Nikki pounded on the door. "I want to talk to you,
Anne," she called.

"Not now," Anne answered. "I'm busy. I've got to
study."

There was a pause and she heard her sisters whisper-
ing. Then another voice, Leslie's silky notes, sounded.
"I've got a date," she called, "and Nikki's going to the library with Mike."

"I'll be all right by myself," Anne yelled back. "Mom
and Dad have been leaving me alone for years if you've
bothered to notice. I keep telling you I'm fifteen years
old!"

Silence.

Anne drank her milk glumly and leafed through the
pages of her algebra textbook. It was a pain in the neck
being the baby of the family. She could remember very
well four years ago when Nikki was fifteen.

Back then everybody had acted as though fifteen was a
very mature age. Even Leslie at fifteen had been treated
with dignity. But when she, Anne, was ninety, they'd still
think of her as needing looking after. She'd always be the
youngest of them all.

No use dwelling on it. Methodically she began to do algebra problems, stopping only to go look out the window on the two occasions when cars stopped out front.

Nikki's boyfriend, Mike, picked her up in his creaking, elderly automobile. With both of them starting college this fall, their idea of a date was a study session at the library.

The second car, a much newer and more expensive one (though not nearly as nice as Jay's Corvette), was driven by one of Leslie's string of admirers. For once Anne was able to watch without envy as her glamorous-looking sister departed on a date.

She went back to stare unseeingly at algebra problems. Each of her sisters was a success. Nikki was a top student, a real brain. She was going to do wonderful things in the world, Anne didn't doubt it for a minute. Her dark pixie look, inherited from Mom, had an attraction all its own.

Leslie took her stunning good looks from their tall, blond father. She'd also inherited his instinctive talent for attracting people.

Anne wasn't a copy of either parent. She was neither small and cute like Nikki, nor tall and striking like Leslie. At five feet five, she was just sort of medium.

Her hair color—brown—was medium too. That was the trouble, Anne decided as she clapped the textbook closed and got to her feet. Everything about her was medium. Medium to dull.

She unlocked the door and crept downstairs in the deserted house. As she'd told Nikki, she'd been left alone hundreds of times before. But somehow, with Mom and Dad out of town, the house seemed so totally abandoned.

Nikki and Leslie were going to try to be so much more bossy than Mom and Dad ever were. If she wasn't careful, the two weeks of freedom were going to be like two weeks in prison.

She was beginning to be hungry now. She searched through the refrigerator, finding the remains of the health-food casserole Nikki had made for dinner. She heated it and ate some with another glass of milk.

Afterward she went back upstairs. She didn't even feel

like calling her best friend, Clarisa, tonight. She wanted to be alone, to think and feel and dream.

Breakfast was toast and juice in the kitchen, while Leslie painted her fingernails and Nikki sat at the table drinking carrot juice and reading a thick textbook.

"If I were you, I'd be making the most of the time before college started," Leslie told her older sister, holding one perfect nail up to examine its paint job.

"That's what I'm trying to do," Nikki answered without taking her eyes from the printed page. "I'm giving myself a refresher course in French composition before I start advanced French this fall."

"That's not what I meant." Leslie sounded disgusted. "I meant I'd be out having a good time before school started. Anne and I have already been in school for a week, we don't have much choice, but you still have several days before college begins."

Nikki looked up, mild surprise in her dark eyes. "But, Leslie, I want to be prepared."

Anne watched her sisters. It never failed to surprise her that the two could be so different. Each was so definite, so sure of what she wanted. Anne wished she could be like that. She sighed.

It was a tiny sound, yet sufficient to draw two pairs of eyes to her face.

"Sorry I came down on you so hard last night, little sister," Nikki apologized lightly.

Leslie's lovely brow contracted into a frown. "But you've got to realize we need to know where you are. And that you can't go around riding with strange boys, even if they do drive expensive sports cars."

The Corvette upset Leslie. Even if Anne had only ridden in it to give directions, Leslie didn't like it.

It was once again typical of the two sisters, Anne thought, that yesterday Nikki was so mad she could hardly speak, but now she'd cooled off enough to be sorry for having lost her temper. And that Leslie hadn't been nearly as mad yesterday, but was still the same amount mad today.

"If you're going to continue to see this boy, you'll have

to bring him over and let us meet him," Nikki continued in a voice that was almost laughable for a nineteen-year-old.

Anne smothered a smile. Nikki was trying so hard to be like Mom.

"For Pete's sake, Nikki," Leslie snapped at her sister, using Dad's favorite expression. "You talk like the child was on a date. A boy who drives a Corvette isn't going to ask her out again."

"He might," Anne snapped back. "And I'm not a child."

"Anne, Leslie," Nikki soothed in her most irritatingly grown-up voice. "Don't quarrel, girls."

Anne gulped down her juice. She felt like she was being smothered. "I've got to get to school," she muttered.

"But it's early yet," Nikki protested, ruffling her short hair worriedly. "You never leave until ten minutes to eight."

"I promised to stop by Clarisa's," Anne yelled, already halfway across the living room, headed for the door. If she let them stop her, no telling what kind of directions she'd be stuck with next.

"Wait!" Nikki wasn't about to let her get away so easily. "Come straight home after work."

"You'd better," Leslie added grimly. "I'm making dinner tonight and I don't intend to hang around here for hours just because you don't know what time to come home."

"What are we going to have?" Anne hesitated at the door to wait for an answer. Having sampled Leslie's cooking on previous occasions, she decided it might be better to plead an invitation from Clarisa's mom.

"Chili dogs and chips," Leslie called. "I thought I'd pick up a bottle of root beer."

"Junk food!" Nikki howled in indignation. "You can't be serious about putting that stuff in your body."

Anne grinned. There went another argument!

She went on out of the house. In spite of Nikki's objections, it sounded safe to come home tonight. Chili dogs might not be particularly healthy, but even Leslie couldn't ruin them.

It was only two blocks down the hill to the Madison home and Anne walked slowly. It wasn't true that she'd promised to stop for Clarisa, but she did so frequently enough not to cause comment.

Early morning hung like a mist over the hills where the small town of Bryan clustered. Birds sang lazily and Anne's heart lifted. What terrible things could Leslie and Nikki do to her anyway? She had to show them she was old enough to make her own decisions, that was all.

And perhaps she'd see Jay again today.

She knew so little about him. She didn't know what school he came from, what his dad was like, what things he liked to do, even what his last name was.

It was all a mystery and it made everything more exciting. The future was still all potential. Anything could happen. Dreamily she imagined herself in his arms, his lips pressed against hers.

"Anne," he said.

No. Anne frowned. That wasn't quite right.

"Anne, darling," he whispered.

That was better. She looked up at him and said . . .

"Good morning, Anne." Mrs. Madison's cheerful voice interrupted her daydream. "Clarisa's still in having breakfast. Why don't you join her?"

"Thanks," Anne said, "but I'm not hungry." She watched Mrs. Madison, who was a gardening freak, carefully push dead leaves and other junk up around the plants in her flower bed.

"We're supposed to have a cold spell tonight," Mrs. Madison explained. "It may frost."

She made it sound like an extremely important event, but Anne found it difficult to be interested in such mundane matters as the weather.

"Is that right?" she returned.

"Do you feel well, Anne?" Mrs. Madison, who like everyone else in Bryan had known her most of her life, peered closer. "You look a little peaked."

Peaked! She'd never felt more wonderful. Indignantly Anne drew herself up. "I feel fine," she answered.

"It's because your parents are away. You're homesick for them. I know how you feel; when I was your age I went to Kansas City to visit my aunt for a week and couldn't eat a thing."

"It's Mom and Dad who've gone away," Anne explained, reasonably enough, she hoped. "I'm still home, so I can't be homesick."

"Then you're not eating properly," Mrs. Madison decided. "Those sisters of yours probably don't bother to cook. Now you march in there and have bacon and muffins with Clarisa."

"I'm not hungry . . ." Anne started to protest, then stopped. "Did you say muffins?"

"Blueberry." Mrs. Madison nodded briskly. "Go on inside and help Clarisa eat them. With just the three of us, we always have leftovers."

Anne told herself she was only doing it to keep Mrs. Madison's feelings from being hurt. She'd always envied Clarisa her only-child status, but she supposed there would be a lot of leftover food in a household of only three people.

When Anne came into the kitchen, Clarisa looked up from the breakfast table with sleepy eyes. "Hi," she said, then yawned.

Anne had known pretty, blond little Clarisa long enough to realize that her sleepy lack of enthusiasm didn't mean her friend wasn't glad to see her. She was simply one of those people who begin to warm up only as dark falls each evening. Clarisa went to bed about midnight and she arose in the morning reluctantly, after much prodding from her mother.

Anne helped herself to a couple of fat, well-browned muffins, spread butter on them, took several slices of crisp bacon and a glass of chilled orange juice.

"What's going on?" Clarisa stared in fascination. "You usually could care less about breakfast. Aren't they feeding you over at your house?"

"I didn't eat much dinner last night. I had a big fight with my sisters." The muffins were delicious, but then the things Mrs. Madison made were always good.

"What about?" Clarisa's sleepy eyes managed to show

a degree of interest. She yawned again, staring at the delicious food with distaste.

Strangely Anne found she didn't want to talk about the new boy in town, not even to her best friend. "I got home late after work and Nikki hit the ceiling. She thinks she's captain of the ship while Mom and Dad are away."

"How awful!" Clarisa's tone was sympathetic. "And you were looking forward to being treated like an adult while your parents were away."

Anne nodded. "Looks like I'm going to have to prove my independence," she said. "In fact, I started last night. You have no idea what it's like to be the baby of the family."

Clarisa sank back, looking depressed. "You should be the only kid," she pointed out. "You get all the attention."

"And all the money and clothes and pretty new bedroom furniture." Anne grinned, not fooled for a minute. "But if you're lonely, I'd be happy to send one of my sisters over."

Clarisa's face took on a look of horror. "Leslie or Nikki? No, thanks."

"Now if we could be sisters," Anne suggested.

Clarisa nodded. "Things never work out that good."

It was comforting to be with Clarisa, Anne thought. They'd been friends since about second grade, but they didn't get to spend as much time together anymore. Clarisa's music had become the most important thing in her life. She played piano, clarinet, and violin, was in both band and orchestra at school, and most of her time was taken up with lessons. Like Leslie and Nikki, Clarisa knew very much what she wanted to do with her life.

It made Anne feel a little left behind at times because all she had was plain old school and her after-school job at Dad's store. She wished she had a talent like Clarisa or Nikki, something that made her stand out, some direction in which she could be headed.

"We'd better get to school," she told her friend, rinsing breakfast dishes and putting them in the dishwasher.

Clarisa left hers sitting on the table. That was another advantage of being an only child, Anne decided: people waited on you. Though Mom said it wasn't an advantage. She said it was good to learn to take care of yourself.

The girls had barely waved good-bye to Mrs. Madison and walked about a block down the hill toward school when something happened to start Anne's heart tingling. She glanced around to see a bright-red car coming from behind them.

If he went by without stopping, she'd pretend she hadn't noticed. Maybe he was only friendly yesterday because he didn't know anyone in town and needed a favor.

Maybe he wouldn't recognize her; medium-sized girls with ordinary brown hair weren't particularly memorable. Maybe . . .

"What a great-looking car!" Clarisa had seen it too.

Anne didn't have to think up a reply because the car pulled to the curb beside them and stopped.

"Hi." Jay leaned out a window. "I went by your house."

"You must have seen my sisters, then." Anne was suddenly shy, not knowing what to say. It was as if she was afraid he'd see inside her head and know what she'd imagined about him.

He shook his head. "I only stopped outside, hoping you'd come out and I could drive you to school."

Clarisa coughed loudly. Both Jay and Anne turned to her. "I don't believe we've met," Clarisa said, looking pointedly at Anne.

"Jay, this is Clarisa," Anne introduced them. "My best friend, Clarisa Madison."

Jay nodded, not saying anything.

"Glad to meet you, Jay," Clarisa bubbled, then flashed her eyes meaningfully at Anne as though to say, You didn't tell me about *him*.

Anne blushed. She didn't want Clarisa making a big deal of this.

"Jay's new in town," she explained. "We met yesterday when I gave him directions."

Jay climbed out of the car to stand with the two girls. He shifted uneasily from one foot to the other and Anne wished she knew how to put him at his ease.

"Maybe I can drive you to school after all," he said.

Anne wasn't sure if he meant just her or Clarisa too, but since she didn't seem to know what to say to him this morning, it was easier to assume he meant both of them.

"Sure," she said. "We'd be glad of a ride."

She squeezed into the one side of the passenger seat that was next to Jay and Clarisa rode on the outside next to the window. While they rode, Clarisa chattered about nothing while Anne tried desperately to think of something to say. Jay concentrated on his driving.

"You must be new in town?" Clarisa asked Jay, even though Anne had just told her that fact. She nudged Anne. "Say something," she mouthed.

Anne shook her head. It was so easy to talk to Jay yesterday, but today she could think of nothing to say.

Finally they reached the school grounds and Jay pulled the car to one side of the street so they could get out.

He must be wondering why he bothered to look me up, Anne told herself. "It was nice seeing you again." She tried to sound bright and sparkling, but even in her own ears the words came out phony.

"I'm so glad I got to meet you." Even Clarisa sounded more like she meant it. She nudged Anne again. "I have to hurry inside because I've simply got to see Mr. Judson before band this morning." Anne understood the nudge. It meant she was leaving the field clear to Anne.

"Wait!" Anne called. "I'll go with you." Right now the last thing she wanted was to be alone with Jay and have to make conversation.

"No!" Clarisa's eyes flashed. "I mean, I need to see Mr. Judson alone and I'm sure Jay wouldn't mind spending a little time with you." She stalked off, not giving Anne an opportunity to accompany her.

Anne looked at Jay. He looked down at the grass. Plenty of kids, standing around waiting for the first bell, would see the Corvette this morning. But even that didn't make Anne feel better.

She was bombing out with Jay. Yesterday had been different. She'd been the Anne she'd always planned to be, the Anne who talked to boys her own age as easily as she talked to old people or little kids. But today was different. The magic had worn off.

"It looks like a nice school," Jay told her, his eyes on the building.

"It's okay," Anne answered. "I hope your dad decides to move here so you can go to this school too."

Suddenly it was easier. She didn't even know why, but it was easier. His smile was warm and honest on her again, more from his eyes than his mouth.

"Meeting you yesterday was the best thing that's happened to me since I came to town," he told her, the words coming out so awkwardly that she knew them to be sincere. He wasn't one of those boys with an oily-smooth line.

"But you'd just gotten here when we met," she teased. "I was probably the first person in town you saw."

"That's not true." He leaned closer to defend himself. "I spent all morning down at the store getting acquainted. I met lots of people, but nobody like you."

"I'm not sure whether that's an insult or a compliment," Anne retorted lightly. Then the words sank in.

"The store?"

He nodded. "Ogden's," he said, "the department store."

Suddenly the truth glowed bright and clear. Mrs. Turner said the Ogden son was in town to look over the local store, but somehow it had never occurred to her he might be a boy only a little older than herself. She'd expected someone at least twenty-five, wearing a business suit and a tie.

"You didn't ever tell me your last name," she pointed out fearfully, hoping against hope.

"And you didn't tell me yours." The truth hadn't begun to dawn on him yet, but then there was no reason it should. Mrs. Turner hadn't been gossiping to him.

"But then I thought it was kind of nice that way." He grinned. "You know, mysterious strangers meet in the night."

She couldn't manage to return the grin. "Afternoon," she corrected. "It was afternoon when we met."

The grin faded as he took in her serious look. "What's wrong, Anne?" he asked.

"My name is Anne Hollis," she told him, waiting to see his reaction. For an instant, there wasn't any.

"Hello, Anne Hollis," he said, then hesitated, the tiniest frown beginning to pucker his brow. "Hollis," he said. "Isn't that the name of . . . ?"

A bell rang in the distance as Anne nodded. "That's right," she agreed. "David Hollis, the manager of the Ogden's in Bryan, is my father. He's the man you've been sent to check on."

All around her, students were moving toward the big front doors of the school building. She had to go or she would be tardy. She blinked back tears. She wouldn't let him see her cry. She wouldn't let him see that it mattered. "Good-bye, Jay Ogden," she murmured. "It was nice meeting you."

3

Not only was Anne not going to let Jay see her cry, but she wasn't about to have anyone inside the Bryan high-school building see the tears either. She dashed them from her cheeks and dared herself to look anything but happy as she marched determinedly through the wide front door.

Inside, everything was perfectly normal. It was the usual controlled chaos of a Wednesday morning in early fall, when the students haven't quite gotten used to giving up their summer's freedom. Anne didn't really listen to the chatter as a surging crowd of kids tried to find lockers, locate books, and get to classrooms at the same time they exchanged vital information with all their closest friends.

Anne wished she were anywhere but here. Most of all she'd like to be home in her own soft-yellow bedroom, trying to figure out why such awful things always happened to her.

But when things are going bad, they usually get worse in a hurry. Leslie breezed by.

"You'd better have a dandy explanation for Nikki about why you were riding around in that red Corvette again when she told you not to," she said, not even interrupting the smile that she was directing at the lead prospect for quarterback of this fall's football team. "She's going to have a fit!"

She didn't even give Anne a chance to defend herself, but swept on down the hall with her friends. It was usually like that when the sisters met at school. Leslie had considered it a personal affront last year when Anne moved from junior high to the high school. Mostly she pretended her younger sister didn't exist.

"Don't listen to her." It was Clarisa. "She's such a twirp. I think Jay's nice."

"So that's why you vanished like that." Anne turned to her friend, trying to smile. "I know very well you didn't have to see Mr. Judson."

"Of course not." Clarisa shrugged, smiling. "I know when I'm not needed. Jay's your guy."

"Not exactly," Anne admitted ruefully. After today, Jay certainly wouldn't be looking for her again, and of course, she never wanted to see him again.

It would be like a betrayal of her father to have anything to do with Jay. Still, the whole thing wasn't the boy's fault; he'd seemed very nice right up to the point when she'd discovered his last name was Odgen.

"Did you really like him?" she asked her friend eagerly.

"Well," the word was drawn out unnecessarily as if Clarisa was trying to think how to answer. "He didn't say much. But he sure does have a gorgeous car," she added hastily, as though that made up for a multitude of sins.

Yesterday the car had mattered a lot to Anne, but today it hardly seemed significant. It was the fact that she probably wouldn't see Jay again that made her feel slightly sick inside.

"He's really special," she protested. "You just didn't get acquainted."

They parted company without Clarisa having been convinced enough of Jay's outstanding qualities to suit Anne. But Clarisa had to report to band class and Anne had to go to English.

Normally it was one of her best classes. The teacher was young, attractive, and knew how to present the material so it seemed alive and interesting. But today her mind drifted in other directions.

Several times she failed to answer questions that would normally have been a snap. When she got up to go to her next class, the girl next to her spoke.

"You're usually a whiz at English, Hollis. Something wrong?"

A boy in back of them tapped her on the shoulder. "Her mind is occupied with other things," he informed the girl. "She's dreaming of expensive sports cars and red-haired strangers."

The girl stared questioningly at both of them. Anne hurried off before she had to explain. Yesterday she would have been glad to have her outing with Jay witnessed, but today she wished it had been secret. But right in front of Bryan High at just before eight in the morning was the opposite of a private meeting place.

All day long comments were made. People were considerably more impressed by the little red car than by the boy who was driving it.

Anne tried to avoid talking about either the boy or his car. Soon everyone in town would know that Jay was here on business—Ogden's business—and that his only interest in any member of the Hollis family was because of the store.

After school, Anne glumly traced the usual three-block walk that led downtown to her job at the department store. As she approached the store, she glanced at her own reflection in the glass windows at her side. Her skirt and blouse still looked as fresh as they had this morning, her brown hair swung as merrily. She straightened her shoulders out of an unaccustomed slump.

Jay might be in the store. She hoped he would be, but at the same time, she was afraid of it.

She breathed easier once she stepped inside and cast a quick glance around. All the clerks were in their usual places, and as was normal at this time of the afternoon, business was in a brief lull.

Nodding greetings at co-workers, Anne stepped briskly toward the clothing department in the middle of the store where she worked with Mrs. Turner.

"Anne," Mrs. Turner greeted her with a grudging smile. "I'm glad to see your teacher didn't find it necessary to keep you after class today."

For nearly a year now, ever since Dad had finally agreed to allow Anne to work part-time in the store, Mrs. Turner had been a test of her patience. Anne had a feeling today was the day she was going to fail that test.

"She didn't keep me after class yesterday," she snapped. "She only wanted to talk to me about my work."

"My, but we are testy today," Mrs. Turner observed, a look of satisfaction on her face.

Anne knew the older woman would like nothing better than to go to Dad with complaints about the one daughter who worked in the store.

She smiled politely. "Actually it's been a lovely day," she lied. "Couldn't have gone better."

She turned away, throwing herself into the work with an apparent enthusiasm that went way beyond the call of duty. Mrs. Turner wouldn't have cause to complain. Dad said he knew the women's clothing department head could be difficult, but he also said that she was good at her business, that Anne could learn a lot from her. Anne doubted it.

She organized and straightened, taking time out now and then for the occasional customer who came into the department needing help. It was close to the end of her two hours when, watching the front door for Jay, she saw an attractive dark-haired girl enter.

Oh no, she thought. Susan Michaels.

"There's that lovely Michaels girl," Mrs. Turner purred. "She came in looking at the new fall clothes after you left yesterday, but couldn't decide on anything."

Anne was well acquainted with Susan. The dark-haired girl was as popular with the sophomore class as Leslie was with the seniors, but though Anne felt there was some defense for her sister, she didn't know of a single good quality Susan possessed.

Don't come back here, she commanded silently. I don't feel up to dealing with you today.

Susan marched straight for junior sportswear, a couple of her friends in tow.

"I'll look after her," Mrs. Turner whispered.

"Nothing I'd like better," Anne whispered back. Moving to a far corner of the small department, she began to straighten a display that had already been thoroughly arranged earlier in the afternoon.

Susan moved into the department like an invading army. "I need something special for the hayride this weekend," she told Mrs. Turner in a sticky-sweet voice that turned Anne's stomach.

It was the kind of voice that really impressed grown-ups. It made them say, "Anne, why can't you have lovely manners like the Michaels girl? Her parents must be so proud of her." As though the Hollis family had to go around apologizing for the way their youngest daughter behaved in public.

"I suppose most of the girls will be wearing jeans," Susan continued, "but I'd like something different. I'd really prefer to go into the city to choose something." This last remark was addressed to her companions. "You know you can't get anything in style or quality in Bryan, but I'll just have to make do." A charming little laugh trilled through the air, evidence of what a good sport Susan Michaels was.

Anne smiled sourly, pleased that Mrs. Turner had to wait on the girl. It was a privilege she'd gladly live without.

"These corduroy pants look okay," she heard Susan say. It was the highest form of compliment Susan could manage for Bryan-purchased clothing.

"Anne has a pair of those on layaway," Mrs. Turner said, indicating her co-worker with a slight nod.

Susan looked at Anne as though just noticing her presence.

"Hi, Anne," she cooed as though they hadn't ignored each other at school that very day.

Her manners were perfectly designed to please the un-knowing and easily impressed adult, but no teenager would be fooled for a moment. Leslie wasn't like that; she genuinely liked people and they liked her in return. But Susan's popularity was a calculated thing.

Anne smiled. She had no choice but to be friendly with a customer. It was part of her job. "I'm sure you'll like those pants," she told Susan, gritting her teeth only mentally.

"Well . . ." Susan hesitated, looking down at the pants as though they'd become less desirable now that she knew Anne Hollis was buying some.

"Hi," the voice spoke from Anne's other side. She turned quickly to face the boy whom she'd been watching for all afternoon.

"I've been busy," Jay explained in his slow, deep voice. He pointed toward the front of the store where Mrs. Wattley, the assistant manager, was engaged in conversation with one of the clerks.

Anne nodded. She knew why he'd been busy. Mrs. Wattley was showing him around the store, explaining how things worked up in the office, giving him a chance to go over every detail of her father's business. It made her burn to think about it. But nothing could be done. He had a right to be here.

"I wanted to ask you why you went off in such a rush this morning," he said, ignoring the others with her.

Susan was unaccustomed to being ignored. "I don't think people should allow their personal problems to interfere with their work," she observed virtuously to Mrs. Turner in a low, but perfectly audible voice.

Anne flushed, but her embarrassment was less than that of the department head. Anne couldn't help but feel a little sorry for the usually unflappable Mrs. Turner, caught as she was between the daughter of one of her wealthiest customers and the son of the store owner.

"I'm sure Mr. Ogden doesn't mean to interfere," she said, hesitating as though certain she'd said the wrong thing. "I mean, Mr. Ogden has a right—"

Jay suddenly became aware of what was going on. "Sorry," he apologized abruptly to Susan. "I'll talk to you when you're through here," he told Anne.

"Ogden!" Suddenly Susan's smile couldn't have been brighter. "The same as the store?"

Jay nodded.

"His father owns the store," Mrs. Turner was only too happy to enlighten Susan. Anne didn't have to bother with introductions. Mrs. Turner introduced Susan and Jay, thinking to include Susan's two friends only as an afterthought.

"You're visiting our town?" Susan edged closer to Jay, her purchases forgotten.

"I'm here on business," Jay told her, his glance still on Anne.

You could have said that before, Anne muttered in-

wardly. It would have saved us both a lot of trouble if I'd
known you were here to spy on my father.

Jay looked at her with puzzlement as though trying to
read the expression on her face. Then they all were looking at her.

"Goodness, Anne. Whatever is the matter? Do you
have a stomachache? You look so grumpy!" Mrs. Turner's voice was concerned.

Anne knew her face must be red. "I feel fine," she answered briefly, trying to sound anything but grumpy.

She watched with dismay as Susan managed to gather a
rather reluctant Jay into her party. Somehow it worked
out that Jay—and not Anne—was included in a group
planning to meet at Ryerson's for cold drinks. Anne had
to admit that Jay didn't fight too hard, but then, what boy
would when the invitation came from such an attractive
girl as Susan Michaels?

Anne watched helplessly as Jay and the three girls
walked away.

"You really should go with them," Mrs. Turner offered
unexpected advice. "It would be good for you to associate
with Susan's crowd, Anne."

"I wasn't invited." Anne turned back to her work.

She didn't want to see anything more of Jay Ogden
now that she knew what he was doing in Bryan, but she
wouldn't wish Susan Michaels on her worst enemy. The
only thing that interested Susan about Jay was the fact
that his father owned the Ogden's chain.

She wouldn't even realize what an unusual person he
was behind that air of reserve. She wouldn't take the trouble to draw him out.

"They would have loved to include you," Mrs. Turner
assured her, "if you'd acted as if you were halfway interested. But when you go all stiff and frozen, it's only natural
they assume you don't want to be included."

Anne stared at Mrs. Turner. Was that how it seemed?
Was she stiff, frozen, and grumpy? From inside, it hadn't
felt that way at all. She'd only felt miserable because the
boy she'd thought could be a good friend—and maybe
more—had turned out to be a *spy*.

"Susan and I don't have anything in common," she answered, because there was no way Mrs. Turner would understand the truth. In fact, she didn't want Mrs. Turner to know how lost and alone she was feeling at this moment. "We could never be friends."

Mrs. Turner marched back behind the cash register and began scanning the daily list of items that needed to be reordered. "You could make more of an effort. You could think of your parents."

Anne leaned across the counter, her brow contracting into a frown. "What do you mean?" she asked, unable to think of a single way her friendships affected her parents.

"If you associated with the right people at school, they'd be drawn into the store. It would mean more business. I'm sure many of the older girls come in here just because Leslie Hollis' father operates the store. But Leslie will be out of school soon and it will be up to you to carry on."

Anne stared in disgust. "Mom and Dad would never expect me to do anything like that."

"I'm sure they don't expect it." Mrs. Turner tilted her attractive head at a questioning angle. "But with the way things are now . . ." She motioned toward the doorway through which Jay Ogden, had departed. "And with both your parents employed by Ogden's, the business is important to your family."

Anne looked thoughtfully around the store. It would seem strange if Ogden's was no longer part of their family life.

She'd wanted to work in the store ever since she was a little girl, and Dad had seemed pleased. Neither Leslie nor Nikki was interested in the business world. Last year, when she was only fourteen, Dad had begun to let her take part.

But maybe it was only because he hadn't the heart to say no. Maybe she did look grumpy and forbidding even when she didn't know. Maybe Mrs. Turner was right and she ran customers off without intending to.

"I'd really hate to see a new manager in here," Mrs. Turner said, looking around the store with a concerned air. "And I would certainly miss your sweet little mother. We all would."

Mrs. Turner was bossy and something of a snob, but Anne didn't doubt her sincerity for a moment. In spite of her faults, she was a loyal and hardworking employee.

"Nobody's fired us yet," Anne retorted, trying to sound cheerful.

Mrs. Turner nodded, looking too dejected to even think of a criticism of Anne. Suddenly she glanced past the girl.

"It's fifteen past six," she said. "You should be started for home already."

Anne turned to look at the clock. Mrs. Turner was right. She tried to smile, even though she didn't feel like it. From now on she was going to go around looking so happy and cheerful that people couldn't help wanting to do business at Ogden's.

"I'd better hurry," she said. "Nikki gets upset when I'm late."

She rushed out of the store and down the sidewalk, not feeling in any mood for another scene with Nikki tonight.

"How about a ride?" a voice called from the street beside her.

Her heart should have sunk at the sound of his voice, but instead it rose with surprising buoyancy, like a bar of Ivory soap tossed into the bath.

"Jay!" she exclaimed, genuinely surprised to see him leaning his head out from the Corvette. "I thought you were with Susan."

"I had a Coke with those girls," he said, looking around to see if anyone was close enough to hear. "But I managed to escape."

Anne couldn't help laughing. Susan was one of the prettiest girls in town, nearly as pretty as Leslie Hollis, which was saying a whole lot. And Jay had chosen to leave Susan to be with her.

"I knew you got off at six," he explained. "Mrs. Wattley told me. I thought you might at least let me take you home."

Anne regarded him thoughtfully. Even if he was a spy, he was here only because his father sent him. He didn't know he was wrecking the lives of her whole family.

"I'm late," she said, still hesitating.

His slow smile spread across his face, lighting up his eyes. "And I do owe you a favor."

Anne got into the car with him, but he didn't start the motor right away. Instead, he looked at her with troubled eyes.

"What terrible thing have I done?" he asked. "Please tell me why you're so mad at me."

4

Anne didn't know what to say. She looked at the boy at her side. His green eyes were troubled.

"It's nothing you've done," she said, impulsively honest. "But more like something you might do."

His forehead wrinkled into a frown. "You're mad at me because of something I might do?" he questioned, then managed a lopsided grin. "Whatever it is, I promise I won't do it."

Anne gave a hopeless little shrug. She supposed that from his point of view the whole thing sounded silly. How did you explain how important the Ogden store in Bryan was to Dad? A boy whose father owned the whole chain couldn't be expected to understand.

"I'm awfully tired," she finally said. "Why don't you drive me home? We can talk about this later when I'm feeling more alive."

The frown came back, but he reached obediently for the controls of the sports car, starting the motor and wheeling the car slowly out into the empty street. "Anything you say," he told her, sounding stiff and formal.

They'd only met a day before, but she knew him well enough already to know what that sound meant. He was hurt.

She was tempted to tell him the whole truth: how Mrs. Turner had implied that he was in town to spy on her father's management of the store and how she felt like a traitor to be friends with the boy who would do such a thing to her own dad.

"It seems kind of funny," she said, trying to introduce the subject without smashing straight to the point.

"What seems funny?" His eyes were on the street

ahead. In another minute they would be at her house. She had to talk fast.

"Funny you would skip school and come out here. You must have had a pretty important reason."

She thought he hesitated before speaking, as though there was something he'd rather not say. "My dad thought it was important," he told her, his voice grim.

She drew in a quick breath. So that was it. His father had told him what to do, he had no choice. But now that he knew her and they'd become friends, it was hard. David Hollis was more than just another employee of his father's chain. He was the father of a friend.

Impulsively she reached out to touch his hand. His position was too much for a boy only a year older than herself. It wasn't fair of his dad to do this to him. "I want you to know you can be honest with me."

His surprised gaze flickered toward her, then lighted on the street again. "I've never felt I could really talk to anybody. My mom died when I was a little kid, I don't have brothers or sisters, and Dad . . . well, Dad hasn't always been a person I could just walk up to and say anything to."

"I hope we can be the kind of friends who can say almost anything to each other," she told him, moving an inch closer to his side of the car.

His smile broke over her like sun from behind a dark cloud. "I'd like that."

He slowed the car, bringing it to a reluctant stop in front of the Hollis home. "You're sure you have to go right in?" he asked.

Anne looked toward the house. Just as she did so, a face appeared in the front window. Nikki!

"No question about it," she told him. "I'm late already and my sister is going to be steaming mad."

"See you tomorrow, then." He opened the car door for her. She stood on the sidewalk watching him drive away before walking slowly toward the front door. Her heart felt light again now that the problem with Jay was cleared up, but when she opened the door, it thudded to the bottom of her chest.

Nikki was still standing at the window, but she turned to look at her youngest sister as she entered the house.

Leslie was seated on the sofa, leafing through a beauty magazine.

For a moment no one said anything and Anne steeled herself for another confrontation. Somehow she had to make Nikki and Leslie see she wasn't a child anymore. She was certainly old enough to come and go as she pleased without everybody making a scene about it.

Perhaps the casual approach would be best.

"Chili dogs ready?" she asked brightly.

Leslie emitted a small shriek and jumped to her feet. "I forgot all about them!" She dashed toward the kitchen. Anne followed her, leaving Nikki to do as she pleased.

A small stream of smoke trickled from the broiler, and when Leslie opened the door, Anne saw that half a dozen blackened hot dogs had sizzled into charcoal. Leslie pulled the pan from under the broiler, setting it on the oven door, while Anne took the pan of chili from the stove.

Thoughtfully she stirred the thickened mass with a wooden spoon. It had stuck to the bottom of the pan. "I'm afraid this is a little overdone, though maybe we can scrape some off the top that isn't too burned." She'd been wrong. Leslie could even ruin chili dogs.

Her sister lifted the hog-dog pan and rushed toward the sink with it. "It's so hot it's coming right through the pan holder," Leslie yelled. She was almost to the sink when the heat forced her to drop the pan, which fell to the floor with a clatter, splashing burned hot dogs all around.

"What a mess!" Nikki shook her head.

"I've burned my hand and you don't even care," Leslie accused her sister.

Anne stepped over the pan and the spilled food to turn on the cold-water tap at the sink. "Hold your hand under this," she said. "That's what Mom always says to do."

Complaining bitterly, Leslie did as instructed while Nikki went to the bathroom for some ointment. After a few minutes of holding her hand under the cooling spray, Leslie turned off the water and examined the burn.

"It's only a tiny little blister," Nikki scoffed.

"It hurts anyway." Leslie took the ointment from her sister and spread it liberally over the injury.

"Who is going to clean up this disaster?" Anne asked, looking around at the shambles of her mother's usually clean kitchen. "And what are we going to eat?"

"We'll all clean," Nikki informed her, bending down with a thick kitchen towel to lift the pan from the floor.

"I didn't have anything to do with wrecking it," Anne protested. "And I'm tired. I've been working."

"I can't do it," Leslie said. "I'm hurt."

Both her sisters glared at Leslie, then advanced threateningly on her from opposite directions. Quickly she sidestepped.

"I have a date," she told them.

"Leslie, dear," Nikki snarled in a meaningful voice.

"I'll call Mom and Dad and tell them," Anne threatened.

"You couldn't do that."

Anne grinned. "Maybe not," she admitted. "But you're going to have to at least help, and then you can take us out for pizza."

Leslie looked doubtfully from one sister to the other. "I could do that," she admitted. "My date's not until eight."

Laughing, the three of them cleaned up the mess. What had started out to be a terrible evening turned out to be fun, with the three of them working together like they used to when younger. Anne wished it could always be like this, three sisters who happened to be a little different in age and a whole lot different in personality. But these days, life with Nikki and Leslie was mostly one big fight.

The kitchen was sparkling again in no time. "Now how about that pizza?" Anne suggested lightly. "I'm starving."

"None of this would have happened if you hadn't been late again," Leslie commented sourly, eyeing her blister. "Don't blame me."

Nikki looked at her pretty middle sister with disfavor. "If you had to come up with an excuse each time you burned something, you'd run out the first week," she told her. "You don't pay enough attention to what you're doing."

"That's true," Anne agreed.

Nikki's attention turned to Anne. "And don't think I've forgotten about you, young lady," she warned.

Young lady. As though she was about four and had been caught getting into the cookie jar. Anne felt her own temper rise, but fought to keep it under control. "I was a few minutes late getting off work," she admitted, "but you know it isn't always possible for me to walk out right at six, not if I'm tied up with a customer or with something Mrs. Turner wants me to do."

"I don't know how you stand that old witch anyway," Leslie murmured, her attention still focused on her injured hand.

"That isn't the point," Nikki said. "And you needn't try to make me think you're late because of work, Anne. I saw you drive up with that boy."

"I got here faster because Jay gave me a ride," Anne pointed out reasonably. "It would have taken me longer to walk."

"Let's go get that pizza," Leslie suggested, as though trying to change the subject.

Nikki stared at her in surprise. "We have to talk to Anne. We're responsible for her. We can't have her running around with every strange boy who comes to town."

"Not many strangers come to Bryan," Leslie argued, reaching for her little clutch bag. She sifted through her makeup to find a small change purse, reached inside, and began counting. "I've only got six dollars," she announced.

"That's not enough," Anne told her. "I'm hungry."

Leslie shrugged. "We'll just have to make toasted cheese sandwiches, then."

"I'll loan you a few dollars," Anne offered reluctantly, "but you have to pay me back."

"Let's go, then." Leslie started for the door and Anne followed.

"Wait a minute!" Nikki yelled, her voice even louder than usual. "What are you two trying to put over on me?"

Anne turned around. "What do you mean, Nikki?" she asked innocently.

Both of the two younger girls were taller than Nikki, but she managed to look fierce anyway. She put her hands against her sides and glared defiantly at them. "You're trying to keep me from asking Anne about this boy she's

been running around with, Leslie, and I don't understand
why. Aren't you concerned about your little sister's wel-
fare?"

"I may be the youngest, but I'm not little," Anne sputtered angrily. "And I'm tired of being treated like a
baby."

Neither of the other girls paid her any attention.

Leslie looked at her watch. "If you want me to treat
you to pizza, we've got to get going. Eric is supposed to
pick me up at eight."

"That's another thing." Nikki didn't relax her pose.
"I've seen the way Eric drives that convertible of his, and
if you've got good sense, you won't get into a car with
him."

Leslie was slow to anger, but her green eyes suddenly
were frosty. "Don't try to tell me how to run my life,
Nikki."

A brown glare met Leslie's, but moments later Nikki
looked down at the carpet. "All right," she sputtered,
"you're old enough to make your own decisions, but with
Mom and Dad away, we have to look after Anne."

"I don't need looking after," Anne interjected, but neither of them listened to her.

"Just because a boy drives an expensive sports car, it
doesn't mean he's good company for a young, inexperi-
enced girl like Anne," Nikki told Leslie.

"I'm not invisible," Anne pointed out bitterly. "It isn't
polite to talk about me as though I wasn't here."

Still they ignored her, looking only at each other. Leslie
lifted one hand in a slight gesture that was like a shrug of
indifference. "Maybe Anne knows what she's doing," she
pointed out.

Shocked, Anne stared at her sister. This was a new de-
velopment, Leslie was on her side! That had never happened before. She'd always stood a better chance at
winning over quick-tempered Nikki.

"What did you say?" she asked, certain her hearing
had failed.

But Leslie kept looking at Nikki, an odd little half-
smile quirking her lips. She glanced again at her watch.
"Let's go eat," she said. "We can talk at the Pizza Place."

A puzzled frown wrinkled Nikki's brow, but she followed Leslie from the house and even allowed her to drive the aging family car. It was the clunker, the second car. Mom and Dad had the good station wagon.

Anne got into the backseat. What was going on? What did Leslie think she knew about Anne?

The girls rode in silence to the pizza spot just outside the little town. The Pizza Place was new to Bryan, and had been hailed by the younger generation as a vast improvement over the more traditional restaurants in the town. As usual, its parking area was crowded with cars, but even so Anne couldn't help noticing the bright-red Corvette parked far to the opposite side.

She knew of only one car in town that looked like that.

Leslie saw it too. Anne could tell by the way she quickly glanced in the opposite direction without saying anything. But Nikki was too busy fuming at her sisters to even look at the automobiles.

"I sure would like to know what's going on here," she said.

A blare of music and conversation enveloped them as they walked into the building, and Anne sniffed appreciatively at the smell of baking pizza.

"I'm starved," she said, suddenly discovering it was true.

Not many tables were empty, but Leslie led the way across the room to a booth in the back, pausing to greet half a dozen friends along the way.

"How can we talk here?" Nikki whispered after they sat down. "With half the high school looking on?"

Anne's heart took a sudden jump when she saw the red-haired boy bent over his pizza in an opposite corner. He didn't look up. He didn't see her. Perhaps it was just as well. She didn't know what Nikki would say if he came over and she recognized him.

They sat down and ordered, debating briefly over what kind of pizza to order. Anne couldn't enter properly into the argument; she was too conscious of Jay, sitting only a few feet away. She wanted him to notice her and yet she didn't.

After giving the order, Leslie slipped over to a nearby

table to chat with friends. Nikki leaned back in her seat, closing her eyes. "I'll be so glad when Mom and Dad get back. I'm not ready for this much responsibility."

Anne stared thoughtfully at her oldest sister. Nikki was no raving beauty like Leslie. People didn't stop and stare at her. But hers was a subtle attraction of softly curling dark hair and large, doelike eyes. She radiated kindness and concern.

But why did she have to act so mean? "Who are you kidding?" Anne asked. "You're loving every minute of this. You like being in charge, even if Leslie and I are perfectly capable of looking after ourselves. After all, nobody made you boss!"

"Someone has to be responsible." Nikki frowned.

"Responsible!" Anne scoffed. "You sure are hung up on that word."

Leslie came back to the table. "I hope they hurry with that pizza." She drummed her fingers impatiently against the table. "I don't want to be late."

"Eric will wait," Anne told her. Boys always were happy to wait for Leslie.

Leslie shook her head. "He's the impatient type."

"Speaking of boys," Nikki interrupted. "I'd like to get back to the subject of this one Anne's been seeing."

"Oh, that." Leslie shrugged dismissal of the topic.

Anne glanced sideways at Jay. He had a book and was reading while he ate.

"We don't know who this boy is," Nikki continued, speaking to Leslie rather than Anne. "We don't know if he's someone Mom and Dad would approve of for Anne."

"Look, Nikki, I know who he is," Leslie admitted, "and for once I've got to admit our kid sister is playing it smart."

Kid Sister? Anne glared indignantly. "You're only two years older than me, Les. That doesn't make you part of a whole different generation."

Then the words sank in. Leslie said she was playing it smart. What did she mean by that?

She didn't have to ask. "What are you talking about?" Nikki demanded.

"If you didn't have your nose in a book all the time

you'd know. Everyone in town is talking about it." Leslie was silenced by the approach of the waitress with their drinks.

Nikki waited until the girl had gone before saying anything. She looked down at her Coke. "I must be out of my mind eating junk food like this."

"Pizza isn't actually junk food," Anne contributed. "I read the other day it actually has lots of nutrition. It has meat, cheese, vegetables, bread—"

"I'm not interested in talking about pizza right now," Nikki informed her in icy tones.

Anne looked around anxiously. Maybe this wasn't a good place to talk. The Pizza Place was crowded with people and Nikki had a way of losing her temper and getting a little too loud.

"I wasn't the one who brought up the subject of pizza," Anne whispered defiantly.

Nikki's attention was once again on Leslie. "You've met this boy?" she asked her sister.

Leslie shook her head and her golden locks moved gracefully, catching the glint of the overhead lights. "If you'd listen, you'd know I said I'd heard about him. Everyone in town knows about Jay Ogden."

"Ogden?" Nikki asked, frowning.

"His family owns the chain," Leslie told her sister. "So you can see why it's important that Anne be nice to him."

Anne, acutely aware that the subject of their conversation sat only on the other side of the room, didn't like the sound of this. "What do you mean, I should be nice to him because of Ogden's?"

"Don't worry, Anne." Leslie gave an amused smile. "I'm on to you. I know how much the store means to you and I've heard the talk."

"What do you mean?" Anne leaned across the table to whisper fiercely.

"Yes, Leslie." For once Nikki was the cool one. "What are you talking about?"

Leslie leaned closer to speak in a low, confidential tone. "The talk is that the Ogden boy is here to check up on Dad and see what kind of job he's doing."

"Dad's a good manager," Nikki replied indignantly.

"Sure he is," Leslie soothed. "But you know how it is in the business world. It isn't always easy to convince the boss that you're doing a great job."

"And Mr. Ogden is Dad's boss," Nikki spoke the words slowly, as though absorbing them.

Anne understood what was going through her mind. They were all accustomed to thinking of Dad as boss at Ogden's. But Jay's father did own the chain.

"Is this true?" Nikki turned to Anne.

Anne stared down at the placemat that listed the sizes and styles of pizza sold at the Pizza Place. "Jay is Jay Ogden," she admitted, "and his dad does own the chain. And he is here on business. He said so."

"People are talking about it all over town," Leslie added. "Everybody's really upset because they say it wasn't fair to' wait until Dad was out of town and then send someone to check up on him. They say this Jay is a spy."

"He's not like that," Anne defended. "He's nice. I like him. And he's only sixteen and has to do what his father says. So it's not his fault."

"Sixteen!" Nikki stared incredulously from one sister to the other, then she laughed. "You think a sixteen-year-old boy has been sent here to investigate the operation of a department store?"

"That's what everyone is saying." Leslie leaned back with an air of injured dignity. "After all, he's not just any sixteen-year-old; he's the only son of the owner of the Ogden chain and people say his dad is sick or something."

"Jay didn't say anything about that," Anne contributed, feeling uncomfortable. She had a nasty feeling she was talking about her friend behind his back, revealing things he'd meant only her to know, but she wanted Leslie and Nikki to have some idea of what he was really like. Everyone was getting a false impression of Jay.

"Don't stick your head in the sand, Nikki," Leslie said in a pitying tone. "You can't pretend Dad's job isn't in danger. Mom's too."

"No one would send a sixteen-year-old for a job like that," Nikki scoffed, laughter still lingering in her voice.

Anne looked from one sister to the other. Which was right? She wanted to believe Nikki was, and that there was no conflict between her and Jay. But Jay was unusually mature for his age, solemn and rather serious. She could imagine a father, especially a sick one, sending a boy like Jay as his deputy.

"I'm sure Jay wouldn't deliberately do anything to hurt Dad."

"Why not?" Leslie asked. "He doesn't know Dad." She grinned, turning back to Nikki. "That's what's so great about Anne's operation. This Jay may not care about Dad and Mom, but he's getting rather interested in their youngest daughter . . . or so I hear."

Nikki's mouth curled in an expression of distaste. "You mean our little Anne is playing Mata Hari?"

"Mata Hari?" Leslie questioned. "What's that?"

Nikki shook her head impatiently. "You mean Anne is deliberately being friendly with this boy so as to influence his report about the store?"

Leslie fluttered her enormously long eyelashes and smiled. "Sure does look that way, doesn't it, dear?"

Talk was silenced once again as the waitress deposited hot pizza in front of them. Usually it was her favorite food, but right now even the delicious smell didn't tempt her. Anne felt sick.

She waited until the waitress left before speaking. She tried to choose her words carefully. "When Jay and I met yesterday, I didn't even know his name and he certainly didn't know who I was."

"Wasn't it lucky it turned out that way?" Leslie commented brightly. "Any good-looking girl in town might have latched on to him."

Anne had time for only a faint shock of surprise that her beautiful older sister was including her among the town's attractive girls. "Jay's my friend," she tried to sound firm. "I don't want to use him."

"Where's your loyalty?" Leslie was aghast. "Don't you care about Mom and Dad? How are they going to feel, coming back so innocently from their first real vacation in years to find their careers down the drain?"

"Really, Les, that's a bit premature," Nikki interrupted.

"It sure is," Anne added hotly.

"Shhhhh," Leslie warned. "Do you two want everybody in the restaurant to hear what we're saying?"

Anne looked around eagerly. Jay was finally stirring from his table. He got to his feet without looking around, plunged one hand into his pocket, and took out some change to leave on the table. Then, taking his check, he headed for the cashier up front. She drew in a breath of relief. He hadn't seen her. She was glad. This certainly wasn't a good time for him to meet her sisters.

She turned her attention back to Leslie. "The pizza's getting cold," she said. "We'd better eat." There was no use arguing anymore with Leslie about Jay. Her sister was convinced she understood the situation and Anne would never be able to make her see the truth.

Leslie took a thoughtful bite. "I do need to get back to the house," she agreed, speaking slowly. But her mind didn't seem to be on her upcoming date with Eric.

Nikki frowned as she sipped at her drink. "Anne, I have no choice but to absolutely forbid you to see this Jay Ogden again."

Anne stared at her sister in openmouthed surprise. "Why?" she asked, too stunned to even be angry.

Nikki bit into her pizza. "You're too young to be involved in this mess. If you go out with the boy, people will say you're being disloyal to your own parents."

Anne frowned. "But you said the whole idea of a boy Jay's age being sent as a spy was ridiculous."

Nikki nodded. "I still think that, though it is always possible, considering he's an only child and all that. But it's beside the point, anyway; you've got to consider what other people will think. You mustn't see him anymore."

Anne turned to Leslie for help. Even if Les did think she was only being a counterspy, at least it was an excuse to see Jay again. She'd known him such a short time, but already an incredible hole would be left if he was no longer a part of her life.

To Anne's horror, Leslie was nodding agreement with Nikki. "She's too young for games like that," she agreed. "If anyone's going to do this job, it should be one of us. And Jay's only a year younger than I am."

"Don't be silly," Nikki snapped. "You know Dad would be furious at either one of you even thinking of such a thing."

"He doesn't have to know," Leslie smiled slowly.

Anne's wrath bubbled over. "You aren't playing a part in some glamorous movie," she informed her sister. "Jay's a real person and he's sensitive and gentle. You can't go around playing with his feelings that way."

Leslie raised her eyebrows only slightly. "All's fair in love and war."

Absorbed in the conversation, Anne had not looked at the crowded tables around them for quite a while, but now she glanced up, hoping no one could overhear the conversation.

To her horror she saw that a tall, red-haired boy was walking from the front toward them. Jay!

Not now. Her heart seemed to stop. If ever there was a bad time for him to meet her sisters . . . But he had seen her and was smiling as he approached.

"Anne," he said. "I was about to leave when I looked back and saw you."

"So good to see you again." She knew her voice sounded false and formal. But if she could just get through this conversation without introducing him to her sisters, if she could pretend he was only some chance acquaintance . . .

He was quick to react to the tone of her voice. The smile faded and a slight stiffness came into his manner. "It's nice to see you again, Anne."

He turned to leave.

"Wait a minute," Leslie commanded in her sweetest voice. She smiled up at the tall boy. "I'm beginning to put two and two together."

Anne closed her eyes. The red hair was a dead give-away. Whoever had talked to Leslie about Jay was sure to have mentioned his appearance. There was no way out.

"Jay." She knew her smile must be as wobbly as her voice. "I'd like to introduce you to my sisters." With one hand she indicated the small, dark-haired girl across the table from her. "This is Nicole, my older sister. Only we call her Nikki. She's going to be a freshman at the university in a couple of more weeks."

She turned to her sister, conscious that she was doing the introduction all mixed up and backward, but not even caring. Conscious of Leslie's stunning eyes, watching and waiting, she wished miserably that she was someplace else.

"This is Jay Ogden, Nikki."

Coldly, barely polite, Nikki acknowledged the introduction. Nobody could accuse her of trying to butter up the boss's son.

Now she had no choice but to introduce him to Leslie. Anne turned reluctantly to her beautiful sister. She looked at Jay and then, with a feeling she was throwing him to the lions, introduced the two of them.

5

The next morning Anne was awakened early by the twittering of birds in the big old cedar outside her window. The sound of the birds was not a pleasant song, but an angry scolding, as if several of them were having an argument.

Sounds like Nikki, Leslie, and me, she thought drowsily, turning over so she could go back to sleep. It was much too early to wake up.

Leslie!

Suddenly the events of the evening before flooded her mind, replaying like a movie inside her head. Leslie was so smooth. There could be no question about that. Jay hadn't even known what happened to him.

Anne sat up abruptly and plopped an angry fist into her pillow. She hoped he had a good time last night going out with her sister.

She turned over and buried her face under the covers, determining to waste no more thought on Jay Ogden. Somewhere in the future she would meet a boy who thought Anne Hollis more attractive than either of her sisters. She'd hoped Jay might be that boy.

Darn! She sat up again. She wouldn't think about him. Two days ago she hadn't even known he existed. It would be easy just to put him right out of her life.

He was a very ordinary boy. Nobody would have noticed him in the first place except for that splashy car. Most people didn't even seem to see how broad his shoulders were in spite of his slimness, they didn't notice his nice green eyes that crinkled in the corners when he smiled. And he didn't relax enough with most people for them to see the sparkle of his grin, his easygoing sense of humor.

Oh! She was thinking of him again. In fact, she'd never stopped. Anne leaped from bed, then moved rapidly across the bare floor. It felt about twenty degrees colder than it had yesterday morning.

She went to peer out the window. It was still half-dark, a wintry, chilly-looking morning. No wonder the birds had sounded unhappy. The grass that looked so summery yesterday looked chill and frosty now. Sometime during the night, winter had made its first inroads.

There! Anne congratulated herself. She wasn't thinking about Jay. Only now she was thinking about him again, thinking how she wasn't thinking about him. It was a vicious circle.

Determinedly she made her mind a blank while she took a hot soapy shower, toweled herself dry, and then dressed for school.

She was surprised when she started downstairs to hear the sound of voices from below. Sometimes Nikki did get up early to study, but normally Leslie slept as late as she possibly could.

"I don't care what you say." Leslie's voice was raised in indignation. "We don't have any choice at this point."

"I won't agree to it," Nikki's voice was even louder. "Anne is my responsibility right now and I won't have her involved."

They were talking about her—and Nikki was using that tiresome word "responsibility" again.

Anne walked into the kitchen. Suddenly the conversation was stilled. Neither of her sisters said a thing, just watched her while she went to the refrigerator, got out the orange juice, and poured herself a glass.

"Everyone's up early this morning," she commented, sitting down across the table from them.

"It wasn't my idea." Leslie sounded grumpy. "Eric called at practically the crack of dawn, wanting to know where I was last night."

"You stood him up, then?" Anne raised her eyebrows questioningly, but tried to keep her voice cool and unconcerned. Of course Leslie had stood Eric up. That's because she was out with Anne's boyfriend.

"Not exactly," Leslie defended herself. "I tried to call him from Ryerson's, but he'd already gone. Anyway, I managed to smooth him over. He's not mad anymore."

"You're good at that." Anne allowed malice to show in her voice, but she tried not to look at her sister.

But she couldn't help seeing that Leslie's expression had darkened. "It's not like you cared about this Jay," she pointed out.

"Not as though I cared," Anne echoed sweetly, determining bitterly that Leslie would never guess how she really felt.

Leslie sipped at a cup of coffee. "Anyway, I bombed out entirely," she confessed. "It was a wasted evening. I might as well have gone out with Eric."

"Really?" Anne realized the question sounded too eager. "I mean . . . what happened? What are you talking about?" She leaned back in her chair as though simply asking a polite question, the answer to which was really quite insignificant.

"I'm glad it worked out the way it did," Nikki's earnest voice interrupted. "It wasn't fair to the boy for you to pretend to be interested in him, Leslie."

Leslie shrugged, her expression sour. "I don't think anybody could hurt that boy," she said. "He's a snob, I guess, not interested in anybody in this town. You could tell he was only going through the motions of being polite to me."

Suddenly Anne's heart sang. "You mean he didn't seem to have a good time with you?"

"That's the understatement of the entire year. In fact, the only topic we could even talk about was you." Leslie turned to Nikki. "I'd try to talk about something interesting and he'd steer the conversation right back to Anne. It was like he couldn't hear enough about her." Disgustedly she shook her head.

Nikki leaned across toward her blond sister. "Leslie," she said, her voice suddenly thoughtful, "it sounds to me like this boy is really interested in Anne."

Anne listened to them, trying to analyze her own

feelings. They were all mixed up. But delight was growing inside her as she realized that Jay hadn't been interested in Leslie.

"Maybe so," Leslie admitted. "That's why she's got to be the one who can see what she can find out."

Nikki shook her head. "That wouldn't be fair to him," she pointed out. "I've told you already that I won't have either of you pretending an interest in him just for Dad's sake."

Suddenly both sisters turned toward Anne.

"I've got to think about this," she said. She got up to walk away, then stopped. "No, I don't," she told them, speaking without showing more than a trace of the bubbling emotion she was feeling inside. "This is my life and I'll decide what to do. You won't tell me."

"But, Anne," Nikki protested worriedly.

Leslie put a hand on Nikki's arm. "Leave her alone," she warned. "She knows what she's doing."

Anne frowned, not liking to leave matters like that. Obviously Leslie thought Anne was going to do what she herself had tried unsuccessfully to do—build up a friendship with Jay so she could get him to influence his father's decision about Dad and the store.

She opened her mouth to speak, then closed it again. It wouldn't do any good. Words wouldn't convince either of her sisters. Abruptly she turned to leave the room.

"Where do you think you're going?" Nikki called after her. "We're not finished talking yet."

"I'm going to school," Anne answered, not even pausing.

"It's too early."

"Then I'll stop by and see Clarisa," she yelled, already in the living room. Anything, any excuse to get out of here and think things through.

The sidewalk, wet with frosty moisture, was slippery under her feet, and the cold wind blew right through her shirt. She'd have to go back inside for a coat. Then she looked up.

A red Corvette sat in the street in front of her house. When she stepped closer, she saw that the boy behind the wheel had his face in a book.

She tapped on the window and he looked up. When he saw who it was, he smiled, reaching across to open the door.

She didn't get in. "Were you waiting for me or my sister?" She was able to ask that question because she was fairly certain of the answer.

The smile faded. He looked serious. "For you, of course."

Still she hesitated. "It's too early for you to take me to school."

"I thought we might take a ride into the mountains and talk," he suggested. "We seem to have a hard time getting a chance to be alone."

Wordlessly she nodded, climbing into the seat beside him. Neither of them said a word until they had cruised slowly out of town, climbing slowly toward the low, bare mountains in the distance.

She glanced at her watch. "I have to be back for school by eight," she warned.

He nodded. "I'll be sure and have you back."

His eyes were fixed on the road ahead. She waited, but he didn't say anything. "You said you wanted to talk to me," she prompted.

"Guess mostly I just wanted to be with you."

A warm glow spread within her. She liked being with him too. How could Leslie say he was boring?

"I was hoping you'd let me take you out last night," he said. "When I saw you in the Pizza Place . . . but instead your sister—" He hesitated as though not knowing how to finish.

"My sister grabbed you and made you take her out," she finished bluntly for him. "The only thing I can say is that Leslie doesn't usually act like that."

He nodded. "I can see she wouldn't need to. She's very pretty."

"Most people say so," Anne admitted. Truth compelled her to continue. "Even I think so."

"She practically insisted I take her over to Ryerson's. Of course, I know why she did it."

"You do?" Anne was surprised. How could he have

found out about Leslie's plan? And if he did know, why wasn't he angry?

They were in the mountains now, an early-morning mist adding an air of expectancy to the heights. Anne looked at the low peaks rather than at him.

"I can see how it would be. You're the youngest. They want to look after you. And they don't know me from Adam."

"That's true," Anne agreed doubtfully, not seeing what he was getting at. "They're extremely overprotective, especially with Mom and Dad away."

Once again he nodded, glancing at her with troubled eyes, then turning once again to the road. "Your sister wanted a chance to get acquainted, to find out if I was the type of person she wanted her little sister to be going around with."

Anne stared at him without blinking. She supposed it seemed logical enough, especially considering that she'd told him from their first meeting how ridiculously her sisters tried to look after her.

Perhaps it was better than having him guess the truth. She certainly didn't want him to know that Leslie's only interest was in influencing the Ogden family to a favorable decision about Dad's management of the Bryan store.

She closed her eyes. She was tired of lies. If only she and Jay could start over right from the beginning and clear things up as they went along. She was sure he would understand.

But no. She couldn't tell him everything now. He would be so hurt. He might even believe she didn't have any genuine interest in him.

"That's it, isn't it?" he probed gently. "Leslie and Nikki were checking me out."

She tried to smile. "Sounds reasonable enough," she admitted, "considering how nutty my sisters act sometimes. But in this case I'll have to admit that I don't know what was going through Leslie's mind. Maybe she just thought you were an attractive male."

He shook his head. "She had to see right off that you were the one I was interested in. Anybody with good vision could see that Leslie and I wouldn't make a good pair."

"You're interested in me?" Anne asked, oddly pleased to have him say it right out in real words like that.

"Sure." His voice was gruff and he didn't even glance in her direction. "You must have guessed that."

They rode in silence for a few minutes. "There's a turnoff just ahead," Anne volunteered. "If you pull over we can get out of the car and look around. From up here you can see the whole town spread down below."

He turned the car off the road as directed. They got out together and strolled to the lookout point. The view was hazy in the early-morning mist and Anne shivered in the cold. He took off his jacket and draped it over her shoulders, then slipped one arm around her, holding her close and warm at his side.

"You can see the roof of our house," she told him, her voice shaking.

Gently he turned her so that she was looking straight into his face. His lips touched hers lightly, soft as a feather against her mouth.

His eyes were questioning, as though he wasn't sure how she would react.

She drew a deep breath. "We'd better go back to town," she told him, hardly aware of what she was saying. "Or I'll be late for school."

Holding hands, they walked back to the car.

Driving back down toward the town, they talked of other things. He told her a little about his dad, who *was* in poor health, and about his apartment home in the city. She talked about school and how mean Leslie and Nikki could be. Neither of them mentioned the instant on the mountain when their lips met in a kiss.

"It's a funny thing," he said as they approached Bryan, "I always thought small towns were friendly. But here I have a feeling people have been talking about me and that they shut up when I come in. Nobody seems very friendly at all."

Anne thought of what Leslie had said. Everybody in town was talking about Jay and why he was here. She wished she could explain, but she couldn't.

"It just takes time," she said.

"I guess." He stopped the Corvette in front of the school.

"See you later," she told him, preparing to get out of the car.

"Wait." He took her books. "Why don't I walk inside with you? After all, I may eventually be a student here myself. I'd like to get a good look at the place."

"Do you really think there's a chance of that?" she asked.

He shrugged. "All depends on what kind of decision my dad makes. But it doesn't hurt to hope."

She was conscious of many looks on them as they walked up to the wide front door. Once there, she stopped and held out her hands for the books. "Thanks for the ride."

"Can't I go inside with you?"

She had no choice but to nod, not even understanding herself why she was so anxious to be rid of him.

The first person they met was Leslie. "Anne," she said, frowning, then noticed her sister's companion. "Jay!" Her voice was sultry sweet.

"Hi, Leslie." He returned the greeting a bit nervously.

"Jay was just walking me to my first class," Anne told her sister firmly, marching on down the hall so that Jay had little choice but to follow.

"Don't let Leslie bother you," she murmured.

"I'll try not to," he replied, "but she acts kind of funny."

"I know."

She spotted Clarisa down the hall. At last, a friendly face to greet Jay.

"Hi, Clarisa," she called. "Wait for us."

A strange expression crossed the little blond girl's face. It was as if she didn't want to talk to them.

"What's wrong, Clarisa?" Anne asked.

"Nothing's wrong," she answered hurriedly. "Hi, Jay."

"Hi," Jay answered.

Nobody said anything else. The noisy conversations around them seemed to emphasize the silence between the three.

"Guess I'd better get you to your class," Jay said, "so I can go to work."

"How are things down at Anne's father's store?" Clarisa asked in a rather pointed manner. "It's a wonderful store, you know, and Mr. Hollis is a terrific manager."

"I'm sure he is," Jay answered, his tone puzzled.

There were no longer any questions in Anne's mind about her friend's strange behavior. Clarisa had heard the rumors and now regarded Jay as the enemy.

She supposed she should be grateful for Clarisa's well-intentioned loyalty, but for Jay's sake she couldn't help being a little mad.

"Come on, Jay," she said. "Let's go."

They walked on down the hall.

"What's wrong?" he asked.

"Nothing's wrong."

"You're frowning. Have I done something to upset you?"

"No." She managed a smile. "It's not you. It's just that I'm going to have a busy day, a test and everything." It was another lie, but just a little one this time. She could hardly tell the truth.

"There's my class," she said, pointing to a door on the right.

Three older boys, seniors in Leslie's class, stood in the doorway. The largest of them, a boy named Rod who played a prominent part on the football team, didn't seem anxious to move.

He looked at Anne. "It's Leslie's baby sister," he said in a voice that was less than complimentary. But he didn't waste much time on her. His gaze went to Jay.

"I don't believe I know you," he said.

Jay was ready to be friendly, Anne could tell, but was also able to pick up on some unpleasant vibrations from the speaker. "Friend of yours?" he asked Anne.

"Hardly." Anne shook her head. "See you later," she said once again, hoping they could manage to simply ignore the senior boys.

"I said I don't know your name," Rod raised his voice as though Jay and Anne were hard of hearing. "But I believe I can guess what it is. In fact, I've heard a whole lot about you."

Anne was fairly sure she knew what he'd heard. "Don't pay any attention, Jay," she instructed.

"Jay!" Rod's tone was triumphant. "That's the náme. Jay Ogden. Your daddy has something to do with the store downtown, Leslie's dad's store."

"Actually it belongs to Jay's dad," Anne corrected.

Rod finally looked at her again. "It isn't right." His tone was reproachful. "You should stick up for your own family."

Jay glanced confusedly from Anne to the boys as if trying to figure out what this was all about.

"Go on, Jay," she whispered urgently.

"No way." Rod frowned. "Jay and I aren't finished talking yet. Are we, Jay?"

Jay didn't answer, but met the larger boy's gaze calmly.

Somewhere in the distance a bell rang and students began to cluster behind Jay and Anne, waiting for the three boys to move so they could enter the classroom.

"I just got one more thing to say." Rod and his friends were in no hurry to move. "We don't need people like you in this town, so why don't you go back where you came from?"

Jay looked at Anne. "People certainly aren't very friendly around here."

"I'm friendly," Rod said. "With the right people." His tone had changed. It had softened, become threatening. Anne felt the small crowd just behind her draw back, heard something like the sound of suddenly indrawn breath.

"I'm friendly," Rod emphasized, taking on a defensive stance. "Are you saying I'm not?"

Anne glanced nervously at the boy at her side. She didn't know what Rod was about to do, but she didn't like the way he was acting. He was something of a bully, a small-town tough who liked to push others around. Jay could hardly know how to deal with a person like him.

"You haven't answered me," the larger boy taunted.

"No," Jay's voice was cold. "I haven't."

That first punch landed squarely on Jay's right eye, but

it was the last move Rod had a chance to make. Jay grabbed his shoulder, spun him around, and before Rod knew what had happened, he was seated neatly on the floor in the middle of the hall.

"What's going on here?" The voice of the principal, Mr. Ryder, sounded suddenly from behind them.

6

Rod stared sullenly down, confused by the sudden upset Jay had handed him. Jay didn't know who Mr. Ryder was; the rest of the crowd of kids melted quickly away. It was up to Anne to answer the principal.

"A little disagreement," she told Mr. Ryder.

"Looks more like a fight to me," he told her. "Not like one of the Hollis girls to be involved in trouble, Anne."

"It wasn't my fault or Jay's," she tried to explain, but he shook his head impatiently.

"That's what they all say. The only thing I know is that I won't have this kind of violence in my halls. This isn't a big-city school!"

"He's from the city." Rod nodded to indicate Jay, then climbed slowly to his feet.

Mr. Ryder looked at Jay. "I don't know you." He scowled. "Are you a new student?"

"No." Jay shook his head. "Not yet, anyway."

"This is Jay Ogden," Anne introduced him.

The principal's eyes narrowed. "Ogden," he said. "I've heard about you. Here looking over Dave Hollis's store, aren't you?"

"You might say that," Jay agreed quietly.

"Dave's a friend of mine," the principal announced with the air of taking a stand.

Oh, no, Anne thought frantically. Here we go again.

"You look kind of young to be involved in business like this." Mr. Ryder peered more closely at Jay. "I heard the Ogden boy was in town, but I didn't expect him to be only a kid."

"Business like what?" Jay questioned, glancing sideways at Anne with an expression that seemed to ask if everyone in Bryan was a little strange.

The halls had emptied as students went on to their classrooms. Anne was afraid her own class was under way. "I'm missing English," she pointed out to Mr. Ryder.

"Oh, yes." He looked from Jay to Rod as though wondering what to do with them. "You go to class," he told Rod, "and I don't want to hear of any more fights you're involved in."

He turned to Jay. "You're not my student, so I guess I can't do anything but ask you to leave. You certainly don't have any business in Bryan High this morning."

Jay looked at Anne. "You'll be all right?" he asked, as though uncertain about leaving her with people who acted so oddly as to attack total strangers.

She smiled weakly. "I'll be fine."

"Pick you up after school?"

"Sure. But you'll have to drive me right to work."

With a nod he was gone and Anne was left alone in the hall with the principal.

"I'd better get to class," she said.

"Just a minute, Anne. I've known you girls since you were babies and I feel about you almost as though you were my own kids. And I think a heap of your mom and dad."

"Yes, Mr. Ryder?" Anne wondered what he was getting at.

"If one of my kids went into the enemy camp the way you're doing, I'd feel betrayed. Don't do this to your dad, Anne."

Without saying another word, he marched back down the hall toward his office, leaving Anne speechless. Indignantly she went into English class, ignoring the curious gazes of her classmates.

She found herself totally unable to concentrate on adjective clauses. How dare everyone in town line up against Jay this way? They didn't know what he was really like. And it was like Nikki said. Who would send a sixteen-year-old boy to judge the work of an experienced store manager?

Still, Jay had said his father was in bad health and virtually obsessed with having his only son become a part of the business. And Jay had admitted just now to Mr. Ryder that he was in town to look over the store.

"Anne. Anne Hollis," the teacher's crisp voice finally penetrated her daze. "Will you please answer the question?"

Anne looked around at the smiling faces of her classmates, then at the indignant one of her teacher. She had no choice but to admit the truth. "I'm afraid I didn't hear the question, Mrs. Snyder," she admitted in a small voice.

"Strange, isn't it?" Mrs. Snyder commented. "Considering you're usually such a good student. If you could only keep your mind on your work instead of sitting there daydreaming about that boy who's trying to take over your father's store . . ."

Was her life the business of everyone in town? Anne could feel her face turning red.

"Jay's not trying to take over the store," she retorted, forgetting where she was and who she was addressing. Did the whole world think she was a child, the baby of the Hollis family, and entirely incapable of showing judgment? "Everybody's wrong about Jay. He's my friend. And I'm inviting him to the sophomore hayride Friday night so all my friends can get to know him!"

She heard a snicker from the back of the room and sank back into her seat, humiliated. This was no place to be making public pronouncements. This was English class!

She stared down at her textbook for the rest of the class, not even looking up as Mrs. Snyder, throwing out the planned study for the day, lectured on Shakespeare's *King Lear*, who it seemed was possessed of some very ungrateful and disloyal daughters.

It had always been pleasant to know her father was so well liked in Bryan, but now Anne began to see disadvantages to his popularity.

She was exhausted with barely submerged emotions by the time the school day ended, and wished she'd never told Jay she'd meet him after school. She almost wished he'd just go away, or at least that he'd not come to Bryan and they'd never met.

She walked slowly away from the front door, looking for the red Corvette.

It was nowhere in sight.

She frowned. Jay's brightly colored car was easy to spot. Even in the crowd of students' autos, it should have stood out. It wasn't there.

She waited impatiently for five minutes, torn between being annoyed and concerned. It wasn't like Jay to be late.

But then, she reminded herself, she'd hardly known him long enough to have a clear picture of what he was like.

She had no choice. She had to hurry or be late for work and get bawled out by Mrs. Turner. She started walking, expecting the sound of a car horn to echo down the street behind her at any minute. Nothing happened.

Mrs. Turner glanced up sourly as Anne entered the department. A customer came in just then, absorbing the department head's attention, and Anne went quietly to work at her usual routine of straightening and stocking. She tried not to wonder what had happened to Jay.

When a familiar face finally appeared in the front of the store, it wasn't Jay's. It was Nikki.

She barely greeted the clerks at the front of the store, heading straight back toward Anne.

"Nicole!" Mrs. Turner fairly reeked of pleasure at the sight of the oldest Hollis daughter. "You must be very excited these days, getting ready for college and all."

Nikki's expression was startled, and Anne guessed that with all the trouble about Jay and the store and trying to look after Leslie and Anne, Nikki hadn't had much time to think of her own life.

"I only wish I was going away to college so I could live in a dorm," she answered, looking glum. "It's tough being the oldest girl in the family."

"Tough!" Anne echoed cynically. "You should try being the youngest. Everyone tries to tell you what to do."

A pained look crossed Nikki's face, as though she'd

heard this particular complaint so many times it didn't even register anymore.

"I came by to tell you Mom called this afternoon, Anne," she told her sister. "Both she and Dad are going to call again this evening and she wanted me to make sure all three of us are there when they call. So you need to come straight home from work," she emphasized.

"Are they having a good time?" Anne asked.

"Great, Mom said. But she sounded a little homesick. I think she'll feel better once she talks to the three of us and reassures herself that we're still alive and breathing."

"Parents always worry, I guess," Anne agreed, wondering why it had to be so. Why couldn't people have confidence in the way you handled your own life?

"They keep thinking we're still little," Nikki said.

"You were such sweet children," Mrs. Turner contributed. "It seems only yesterday."

"Seems a lot longer than that to me," Anne said.

Nikki cast a glance at Mrs. Turner. "The thing is that Mom and Dad want to know if everything is all right," she told her sister.

"Oh, dear." Mrs. Turner looked worried. "Perhaps you should tell your parents about the Ogden boy being here. They might want to rush right back and look into this matter, protect their interests, you know."

Anne could see the annoyance in Nikki's expression. Nikki wasn't used to the way Mrs. Turner considered Ogden's and the Hollis family to be a part of her own personal business.

"Tell them everything's fine," Anne suggested. "No need to spoil their vacation. They'll be back in a little over a week anyway."

"A great deal can happen in a week." Mrs. Turner sounded ominous.

"I do feel a responsibility to keep them informed." Nikki took on a worried look.

"Responsibility!" Anne scoffed. "That's your favorite word. Everything's fine here and there's no need to get Mom and Dad upset over nothing."

Nikki stared at her younger sister as though trying to

see right through her. "No matter what I do, Anne, I'm only thinking of what's best for you."

Anne turned away, frustrated and angry. Why did the whole family have to keep treating her like she was a little girl?

She stalked away to the three-way mirror where customers could view the clothes they were considering buying. She looked at multiple images of herself.

Anne Hollis, fifteen years old, short dark hair, blue eyes, a slender figure. Jay said she was attractive. She certainly didn't look like a little girl.

Fortified by the sight of her own reasonably grown-up appearance, she turned and walked back to where Mrs. Turner and Nikki watched with puzzled expressions.

"If it comes to a vote, I say we don't tell Mom and Dad. Let them at least have a good time before—well, before whatever happens."

"I'll think about it," Nikki promised, sounding as though it was her decision alone.

It was true, in a way. Any one of the Hollis girls could break the silence and tell their parents about what was going on in Bryan. It gave Anne a feeling of power to realize that. If she wanted to talk, she didn't have to worry about Nikki or Leslie's decisions. Tonight on the phone she could start in and tell Mom and Dad all about it. She could get her version in first so they wouldn't be prejudiced against Jay before they even met him.

"I'll think about it," Nikki repeated, preparing to leave. "Don't forget to be on time," she warned again. "And it's your night to fix dinner."

Anne had forgotten about that. But she wasn't about to admit it. "I'm planning something special," she said, wondering what on earth she could make without much advance planning.

She watched her sister walk from the store, continuing to stare at the doorway even after Nikki left. Any minute now, Jay might walk in.

No such luck.

"Guess I'd better get back to work," she finally said, trying to sound cheerful.

Mrs. Turner nodded abstractedly. For once she didn't

seem to have any criticism of Anne. "I do urge you to tell your parents about this situation," she said. "Ogden's wouldn't be the same without them."

Anne tried to decide what was the best thing to do. She worked through the rest of the afternoon, her hands busy and her smile ready for customers, but her mind was occupied with the problem of what to say when Mom and Dad called.

Once again she kept looking for the red Corvette to show up as she walked home. It didn't.

She felt extra tired as she walked the last few steps toward home. She opened the front door and went inside.

"Here she is now, Dad," she heard Nikki say.

"Come on, Anne," Leslie called. "It's Mom and Dad."

Leslie motioned her into the kitchen, where she was talking on the wall phone. Anne took the receiver from her sister.

". . . and that's how it's been, Dad." She heard Nikki's voice and knew she was on the extension.

"Hi, Dad," Anne said, her voice sounding dull even in her own ears. Here she was, talking to Dad, and she still hadn't decided how much he should be told. She hadn't even decided what they were going to eat for dinner!

"Hi, baby," Dad's mellow voice sounded in her ear. "Your sisters treating you right?"

That was a question she hadn't anticipated. Anne glanced at Leslie, innocently waiting her turn again.

Now was her chance to tell Dad all about how domineering Nikki had been acting, to tell him about the wild plans Leslie was hatching. She'd give him an earful.

"Anne?" Dad's voice sounded again. "Are you there?"

"Yes, Dad. I'm here," Anne answered. "I just got home from work."

She stared doubtfully at Leslie. It was so tempting, but somehow it didn't seem quite fair. It was like when they were little kids. This would be like running to Dad yelling that Leslie had hit her or Nikki had taken a toy. They weren't children anymore. This was a problem they had to work out for themselves.

"Things okay between you and the girls?" Dad asked again, a shading of doubt in his voice this time.

"Sure, fine. I'm making dinner tonight."

"Make something good," he told her. "Your mom wants to talk to you now."

"Hello, Anne?" Mom's voice, light and distinctive, came through. She sounded frivolous and happy as a girl.

"Hi, Mom." Anne tried to take some of the lead out of her voice, but it was hard to pretend to be cheerful. "I miss you."

"We miss you too, darling. Are you sure you're all right? Is Nikki taking good care of you?"

"I'm fine, Mom," Anne answered indignantly. "And I don't need Nikki to take care of me."

"Of course you don't," Mom answered indulgently. "I keep forgetting you're almost grown up."

Anne tried not to sigh. This was the heart of the problem.

"I've already talked to your sisters, so I suppose I'd better go. Your father says the phone bill will be astronomical."

This was her last chance to talk about the problems at the store.

"Mom, I've met this boy," she blurted out.

"That's nice, dear. Someone special?"

"Special," Anne echoed. It sounded dumb. "He's all right, I guess. He's new to Bryan. His name is Jay."

"Jay?" The way Mom said the name it was a question.

But suddenly it was a question that Anne couldn't answer. Mom and Dad sounded so happy, like two kids on a holiday. She couldn't ruin their fun by embroiling them in the trouble here at home. And maybe there wasn't any real trouble at all. Anne couldn't believe Jay would deliberately do anything to hurt her father. Though there was no telling what Mr. Ogden had in mind.

"Tell me about Jay," Mom said, interrupting Anne's thoughts.

Anne tried to think how she would describe the newcomer to town. She could say he was tall and broad-shouldered, that he had red hair and drove a Corvette.

But none of that was really Jay. She was suddenly shy, as if by putting Jay and her feeling for him into words she would be saying too much and it would all vanish like smoke blown into strong wind.

"There's not much to say," Anne answered. "I only wanted you to know."

She let Nikki and Leslie say good-bye, going over to peer into the refrigerator on the pretense of choosing something for dinner. There wasn't much point in telling Mom about Jay, even if she could have come up with the right words, because he seemed to have disappeared from her life this afternoon.

Leslie hung up the receiver with a decisive click. "What's for dinner?"

"Tacos." Anne made the decision even as she spoke.

"You didn't defrost the meat."

"It'll defrost in the pan while I'm cutting up the lettuce and cheese and stuff."

"I can't be late. I have a date with Eric and he's not feeling too patient with me these days."

"Why worry?" Anne asked, taking a package of hamburger from the freezer. She put it under running water in the sink to begin the defrosting process while she got out a pan and wooden spoon. "You've always got a long line of boys waiting to take you out."

"Eric's different." Leslie's voice didn't change, but she looked away.

Anne looked at her curiously, wondering what it was like to be as beautiful and popular as Leslie, to have your pick of most of the boys around. Maybe it wasn't so different. Eric was the one who counted.

Anne decided she wouldn't trade Jay for a whole line of boys, if she ever saw him again.

It took nearly an hour to prepare dinner because of the frozen meat, but finally they sat down together around the kitchen table.

It looked nice, the silverware neatly in place, napkins folded beside the plates. Nikki glanced approvingly at it.

"This looks good," she said. "Almost like having Mom and Dad home again."

For just an instant Anne knew what it would be like to feel homesick for her parents. It wasn't that she wasn't glad they were off having a good time, only everything seemed to have gotten so muddled since they left. She missed Jay and wanted to know where he was right at this minute. Maybe he'd gotten tired of the whole attitude in Bryan after the scene in school this morning and had packed his bag and gone home.

Not without saying good-bye. Anne couldn't believe it. She blinked back tears. Don't cry. Only babies cry.

"Tastes good too." Leslie ate hungrily. "It's been such a cold day and this spicy food helps warm me up."

She was the only one eating. Nikki stared down at the table, looking as if she'd lost her appetite.

Anne stared curiously at her oldest sister. What was Nikki so depressed about? She should be having a ball going around pretending to be in charge of everything.

Anne imagined what it would be like to be Nikki. Everyone in town respected her brains and she was pretty, too. It wasn't fair.

In another week or so she'd be attending classes at the college up on the hill. No doubt she'd do terrific there.

No, Nikki hadn't a thing to be depressed about.

"I'm not hungry." Nikki put her fork down and got to her feet. "I'm going to my room."

"You're missing a good meal," Leslie told her, washing down the hot food with an iced drink.

Nikki didn't even make remarks about junk food. She hardly seemed to hear what Leslie was saying. Her eyes, large and sorrowful, were on Anne.

"You know I wouldn't do anything on purpose to hurt you, Annie," she said. "You know that, don't you?"

Anne considered. "I guess not," she admitted doubtfully. It was true. Most of the time the damages Nikki did were through a mistaken idea of looking after her.

"I try to do my best," Nikki commented, as though trying to explain some action she'd taken. She went out of the room and they heard the sound of her footsteps going upstairs.

Leslie frowned in the direction in which she'd vanished. "That was weird."

Anne raised her eyebrows. "I thought you might have some idea what she was talking about."

"Not me." Leslie pushed her plate aside with a contented sigh. "In fact, tonight I'm not wasting time worrying about anything. Eric and I are going to drive over to Marfa to hear a live band and we're going to have a good time. I'm not even going to think about a problem."

"Don't forget what Nikki said about Eric's driving," Anne reminded Leslie absently. "Make sure he's careful."

Leslie made a wordless sound of disgust. "Watch out, kid," she warned. "Or you're going to get to be just as bad as Nikki."

Anne grinned. "Sorry."

After Leslie went up to shower and change, she began to slowly clear the table. From time to time, she glanced at the telephone. Maybe Jay would call.

Surely, surely if he was able, if something was not terribly wrong, he would call.

But even by the time the kitchen was sparkling clean once again, the phone hadn't rung. Impulsively Anne walked over to the silent instrument.

It took only an instant to skim through the skinny Bryan phone book. She dialed Mrs. Fumble's number.

"Hello?" She recognized the woman's voice on the line.

"Mrs. Fumble." Deliberately she didn't give her own name. "May I speak to Jay Ogden."

There was a hesitation as if of disapproval on the other end of the line. "Anne Hollis," a middle-aged voice scolded her, "in my day a young lady did not call a gentleman."

Anne sighed. She refrained from pointing out that this wasn't Mrs. Fumble's day—in fact, it probably wasn't even her century! She might have known there would be no way of remaining anonymous in this town. Mrs. Fumble had recognized her voice immediately.

"Mrs. Fumble," Anne tried to sound firm, "please let me talk to Jay."

"I'm sorry." Mrs. Fumble didn't sound as though she was truly sorry at all. "But he went away. He left at about ten o'clock this morning."

Ten o'clock. Not long after the scene at school.

The sound went dead on the line and Anne knew Mrs. Fumble had hung up.

7

The next day was cold and windy, but that didn't keep the members of the sophomore class from talking about the hayride planned for that evening.

"I can't wait to meet your new friend," a classmate told Anne. "I've sure heard a lot about him."

"I've already met him." Susan Michaels spoke with a knowing smile. "But I'm looking forward to getting better acquainted. I suppose Anne has the inside track, though, and he has to take her, since her dad is an employee."

"Dad doesn't work for Jay," Anne wasn't able to keep from retorting. Something about Susan's silky voice made her want to argue.

But she knew she should keep her mouth shut. Jay was gone. He didn't even know about the hayride she'd planned to invite him to.

She wondered if she should start making excuses now, say her head or her stomach hurt, just to sort of lay the foundation so nobody would be surprised when she and Jay didn't show up tonight.

"Anne has the right to invite anyone she wants," Clarisa defended her friend loyally.

Anne managed to smile. It was nice of Clarisa to try to defend her, particularly when she felt the same about Jay as everyone else did.

It was such a cold day that Clarisa's mom picked her up after school, offering Anne a ride to the store.

Anne shook her head. "I'm not working today," she said. "I arranged to take the afternoon off because of the hayride."

"Then how about a ride home?" Mrs. Madison smiled. "It's too cold to walk."

Anne got into the car. She didn't care what she did. Walk or ride, it didn't make much difference.

"What's wrong, Anne?" Clarisa asked. "You look a little pale."

"It's my head," Anne decided quickly, seizing at the opportunity. "It hurts."

"Oh, dear." Mrs. Madison's placid face took on a look of concern. "And your parents are out of town. Perhaps I'd better take you right to the doctor."

Anne had forgotten to calculate the overconcern that the parent of an only, extremely healthy child can feel. She glanced sympathetically at Clarisa.

"No." She shook her supposedly aching head. "I'm sure it's nothing serious."

"I know what it is," Clarisa sounded grim. "You're upset because everyone's been giving you a bad time about Jay." She leaned toward the front seat, speaking to her mother. "They've been perfectly awful to Anne, Mom, because she's dating the Ogden boy."

"Oh." Mrs. Madison sounded startled. "You mean the one who's here about the store?"

Oh, no! Not sweet Mrs. Madison, who never listened to gossip. It seemed to Anne that everyone in Bryan was interested in her private life. At least they didn't know yet that Jay was no longer part of that life. That he'd packed up and left town without even a good-bye.

They stopped in front of the Hollis home. "Just don't let anybody push you around," Clarisa instructed, sounding really mad now. "You just bring Jay to the hayride and have a good time in spite of them. I haven't stood by you very well so far, but I'll back you up from now on."

"Thanks," Anne answered doubtfully. Then she walked slowly toward the front door. This evening was going to be awful.

She knew now what she had to do. She had to get ready, just the way she'd planned, and go by herself.

She would tell them she would have brought Jay, but they had driven him away.

It would be dreadful, but it was the only thing to do. She owed Jay that much.

Nikki was the only one at home. She was sitting in the living room, holding a book in her hands, but staring vacantly at the front window.

"Anne!" She jumped guiltily. "I didn't expect you home so soon."

"Mrs. Madison and Clarisa gave me a ride."

"That's nice." She hesitated. "Anne, I haven't seen the Ogden boy around in a day or so."

And you're glad. Anne didn't speak the accusation aloud, but it was because she knew Nikki would be pleased to know that Jay was gone for good. She didn't say anything, but began unbuttoning her coat.

"You never know about a boy like that," Nikki went on. "He might just take off without saying a word."

Anne frowned at Nikki. Her sister sounded so nervous and she was chattering on and on. What did she know about Jay?

Nikki didn't meet her eyes. "I mean it's not like with the boys around here. We've known them since they were little. We know their parents. We know what to expect."

Anne didn't say anything. She put her coat in the hall closet.

"I made some carrot cake," Nikki offered. "I know you like carrot cake."

Anne didn't know what was going on, but somehow she felt like the carrot cake was either a bribe or a peace offering. And she didn't even know what Nikki had done.

"I'm not hungry," she said. "Anyway, we're going to have hamburgers out at the Michaels ranch after the hayride."

"You always like carrot cake," Nikki sounded as though her feelings were hurt. "I made it just for you."

"I'd better go up and do my homework." Anne edged toward the stairs, anxious to get away from this strange-acting Nikki. "I want to have plenty of time to get ready."

The homework went slowly; she couldn't keep her mind on it. All she could think of was Jay and the hayride. It would have been such fun with him, but now it was going to be the worst evening of her life.

It was beginning to darken already by five-thirty, but

the wind had died down and she knew the night would be sparkling and cold, perfect for the outing.

Instead of her usual quick shower Anne took a long, relaxing hot bath, complete with a generous amount of the scented bath crystals Leslie had given her for Christmas. She had a feeling of needing to put on her best armor for this evening. She could well imagine what choice remarks Susan Michaels would hurl in her direction.

She dressed slowly, pulling on the tan corduroy pants she'd gotten out of layaway for the occasion, and the matching earth-tone plaid blouse. She brushed her hair until it was a glowing cloud of darkness and touched her lips with gloss. Usually her vivid coloring kept her from needing other makeup, but tonight Clarisa was right. She looked pale.

She was about to go borrow some of Leslie's cosmetics when the doorbell sounded from downstairs. She waited for someone to answer, but it sounded again. And then, after a wait, it rang once again.

Anne frowned. She knew Nikki was home. Why didn't she answer the door?

She started downstairs. Nikki was standing in the living room and she turned guiltily at Anne's approach.

"Who was that at the door?"

"Oh, just—just someone looking for another house. It was a wrong number—I mean, a wrong address." Nikki laughed nervously.

"I thought you'd never answer it." Anne turned to go back upstairs.

The doorbell rang again.

She turned, her eyes narrowing. "You didn't answer it," she accused, not understanding why the usually collected Nikki was behaving so strangely.

She walked across the room and flung the front door open.

It was Jay.

She had imagined him calling or coming by, standing there looking at her like this, for so many hours that now she couldn't believe it.

He smiled at her as though nothing had happened, as

though he'd shown up right on schedule. She was tempted to slam the door in his face.

"I'm back," he told her happily.

Angrily she stepped closer and then she saw the dim bruised-looking circle around his eye where Rod had hit him.

Her anger cooled slightly. He had a right to be mad, but not at her.

She turned around, looking to Nikki for support, but her sister had vanished.

"Can I come in?" he asked. "It's chilly out here. And I'd like to talk to you."

"Come in." She stepped back to let him enter. "I want to talk to you too."

Instead of stepping past her, he moved closer and she thought for a moment that he was going to put his arms around her. She stepped back hurriedly.

"Sit down." She indicated the rust-colored sofa, seating herself across the room from him.

Her disapproval must have been evident because a puzzled look came into his eyes. "What's wrong, Anne?" he asked gently.

Such a stupid question to ask! Did he think he could just disappear for two whole days and have her think nothing of it?

"Nothing's wrong. I was just getting ready to go out."

He looked at her, seeming to take in the new outfit. "You look very nice."

She wanted to scream. Couldn't he see that at the very least she had a right to some sort of explanation for his disappearance? But screaming wouldn't do any good. If it didn't occur to him that she'd been worried and upset, forcing him to apologize wasn't going to make a difference.

"I see you have a little souvenir of your visit to school yesterday morning," she commented lightly.

His hand went to his face. "My eye, you mean?" He grinned. "Dad asked me about that. He said he knew growing up in a city neighborhood could be tough, and that was why he'd insisted I take training in self-defense, but that it took real effort to get into a fight in a small friendly town like Bryan."

"Friendly." Anne repeated the word glumly. Usually Bryan was a friendly place. "You've seen your father, then?" she inquired politely.

A frown rippled across his face. "Of course. Didn't Nikki explain when she gave you my message?"

Anne whirled to look again in the direction in which her sister had vanished. No wonder Nikki had acted so funny. "Message?" she queried.

He nodded, looking puzzled. "I called the house yesterday morning to tell you there was a message for me to come home immediately. I was afraid Dad was having another heart attack. That's what the doctors thought, too, and that was why they hospitalized him so suddenly—"

"Wait a minute." Anne tried to slow him down. This was too much information to take in so suddenly. "You mean you had to rush home because of an emergency and you still took time to let me know?"

"Sure." He nodded again. A wisp of red hair fell across his forehead and he brushed it back with one hand. "I wouldn't have left without letting you know. Of course, I didn't give Nikki all the details. I only said I had to get home because Dad was sick. She probably thought he had the flu or something like that." He tried to smile.

Anne got up and went over to sit on the sofa beside him. "He's got a bad heart?"

Jay looked down at the glass-topped coffee table in front of him. "He had a major heart attack last year. The doctors say he was lucky to recover and he's got to change his life-style from now on." He lifted his shoulders in a shrug. "He's always driven himself so hard, it's tough on him to try and change now."

Anne regarded Jay with open sympathy. He'd lost his mother as a child and his father's health was delicate. No wonder he seemed serious and even somber sometimes. "But you said it wasn't a heart attack this time?"

He looked at her, relief evident in his eyes. "It took a lot of tests to find out," he explained, "but they say he only needs to get away and take it easy for a while. But he won't do it; that's why I talked him into coming back to Bryan with me. This mountain air will be good for him. I got him to go out fishing today."

"That's good," Anne said. This explained a lot about why a sixteen-year-old boy had been sent to Bryan. His father must really depend on him.

Jay regarded her with a puzzled look. "I still don't understand. What did Nikki tell you about our conversation anyway?"

There was nothing to do but tell him the truth. "She didn't tell me a thing."

"You mean she said I'd called and would be away and nothing else?"

Anne hesitated. It would be hard to explain why Nikki would pull such a dirty trick. "She didn't even tell me you called, Jay," she explained gently.

His gaze searched her face as though he was trying hard to understand. "But you must have thought—"

"I couldn't imagine what to think. I was worried and mad and everything else. I even called Mrs. Fumble, but she only said you'd gone away and I thought it was forever."

They sat in silence. Somewhere upstairs something fell to the floor. Nikki must be up in her room. Grimly Anne set her jaw. There was no excuse for what Nikki had done.

Clumsily Jay reached across to take her hand. "I wouldn't go away forever," he told her, "not unless that was what you wanted."

Anne swallowed hard. She squeezed his hand, then pulled away. She got to her feet and walked rapidly to the other side of the room. "It's a good thing you showed up when you did," she said, feeling the moment was turning a little too serious. " Or you would have missed *the* event of the social season in Bryan."

"We couldn't have that." His eyes followed her. "And what is this big event?"

"The sophomore-class hayride. And I bragged to everybody that I was bringing you."

"You want me to go with you?" He sounded pleased. "Tonight?"

"Right now," she assured him breezily. Then another thought occurred to her. "If your father doesn't need you."

He shook his head. "Dad was going to watch an old movie on television, then go to bed early. I'll give him a call so he'll know I won't be in until late." He hesitated. "If you're sure you want me. I don't seem to fit in with your friends, no matter how hard I try."

"Don't worry about that. This evening is for the two of us. We won't even notice if anyone else is there."

It was easy to pretend there was no one in the world but she and Jay as they drove together in his car out to the Michaels ranch, but once they climbed into the big hay wagon, pulled by horses, it was a little harder.

Anne found a place for the two of them near the back of the wagon and together they scooped out a little nest in the sweet-smelling hay, then spread the blanket that Anne had brought with her. They sat close together and Anne leaned her head against his shoulder as the horses began their *clip-clop* pace out of the ranch yard.

Only a dim light shone from the front of the wagon and the figures of the other riders were vaguely outlined by the silver of the moon and the distant, sparkling stars.

It was cold, but still and beautiful, the air dry and chilled in the mountainous ranch setting.

"I'm not sure I'd trust this vehicle on a crowded highway," Jay whispered.

Anne laughed softly. "Not many crowded highways in these parts, stranger," she drawled. Then she added in her natural voice, "Don't worry. We won't even leave the ranch. Susan's parents are putting on this private hayride just for us. We have to take turns with the wagon and horses, though, so everybody gets a chance to ride; we'll only be out about thirty minutes."

"We'll make the most of it." Almost shyly Jay took her hand, holding it in both of his own.

Neither of them said anything. There was a closeness between them that made words unnecessary. Anne knew she could never feel quite alone again.

"I missed you while you were gone," she whispered.

"Me too," he murmured. "I mean, I hated being away from you."

It was as if the old wagon, drawn by a horse along a rugged ranch road, was a ship at sea. Anne knew they weren't alone in that ship, but she knew too that the other passengers wanted the same privacy of dark night and sweet-smelling hay.

The ride out was a quiet twosome time. Anne huddled within the closeness of Jay's embracing arm. She wondered if he would kiss her again.

After a fifteen-minute ride, the big old wagon turned around and headed back. With the turn, the mood of the party seemed to change. People began to sing old favorites, songs like "Row, Row, Row Your Boat" and "Working on the Railroad." They even sang "Jingle Bells."

"It's a long time till Christmas," Clarisa scoffed from near the front of the wagon.

Anne understood it. There was a Christmasy feel in the air. Maybe it was because riding in a horse-drawn wagon reminded them of the open sleigh in the song, but she thought it was more than that. It was the feeling that something wonderful might happen.

She wondered if the others felt it too. "Do you feel especially good tonight?" she asked Jay, careful to keep her voice low. It wasn't a question she wanted everyone to hear.

He chuckled, a low throaty sound. "I always feel good when I'm with you," he said. "You should know that by now."

"No." She was impatient with compliments. "I mean, really."

He pulled her closer. "Let me put it this way. This town has been trouble since I first couldn't find my way around in it. My landlady tells me what to do, a boy I've never seen before punches me, and your sisters, both of whom are slightly strange, hate me. Surely you must have some idea why I'm sticking around."

Now it was her turn to laugh.

"What's so funny back there, Hollis?" a voice called from somewhere in the middle. "Didn't know your boyfriend was a comedian?"

It was a teasing remark, not a deliberately unkind one. Most of the kids on the wagon were good friends, classmates from years past. They might not approve of Jay or his presence in their town, but they tolerated him tonight for her sake.

Maybe this was the chance for them to see what he was really like. She did so hope he would come to like it here. She tried to remember what the two of them had been talking about.

Oh, yes, all the things that had gone wrong for him in Bryan.

"Nikki and Leslie aren't so bad when you get to know them," she defended, hardly knowing why she should be saying something good about her sisters.

"I don't think they want to know me," Jay retorted. "At least, Nikki sure doesn't."

Anne was still going over the last part of what he'd said. "You're sticking around because of me?" she asked, suddenly feeling a little shy with him. It was one thing to be friends, but they'd known each other such a short time for this . . . whatever it was . . . to be happening.

"Because of you," he assured her, his voice husky and solemn.

It scared Anne a little, that seriousness in his voice. She'd had it all planned out. She would have boyfriends in high school, dates to go places and have fun with, but nothing serious for years and years, probably after college.

It was not time yet to really begin to care about a boy. Could she be in love after only a few days?

In love! The two words, spoken only in her own mind, reverberated throughout her being.

"Do you believe in love at first sight?" she asked him dreamily.

He thought for a minute. "No." His answer came as a shock. "I don't think so."

The cold practicality of his reply doused her romantic feelings like cold water poured on flame. She pulled away from him.

His mind was still logically considering her question. "It seems to me that any feeling a person *thinks* he feels at the first meeting has to be based purely on appearances."

"Appearances! You mean just because somebody's terrific-looking?" She thought of Leslie, who certainly convinced a lot of boys that they were in love with her.

"Sure," he agreed. "And that isn't love."

"It isn't?" Somehow this conversation wasn't going the way she thought it would. "You mean people just imagine they're in love?"

"Sure," he agreed again. "How could you really know what the other person was like at that first meeting?"

Why did he have to be so logical? Anne turned her face away from him and, concentrating on the song being sung by her friends, contributed her own soprano to the music.

They were back at the ranch house and the wagon drawn to a stop before she spoke another word to Jay. "Let's get down," she said, her voice cold.

"What have I done now?" he asked indignantly.

Clarisa was just ahead of Anne as they climbed down from the wagon. "I told you, Anne," she whispered.

"You told me what?" Anne whispered back.

"Maybe I didn't actually tell you," Clarisa said quickly, glancing back over her shoulder at Jay, who was still waiting up on top of the wagon. "But he isn't the kind of boy you should be going around with."

Anne didn't reply, but waited for Jay to join her on the ground. Clarisa could be right. He was insensitive and unaware.

"What's wrong?" Jay asked again, not seeming to care that other people, people who would be pleased to see them quarrel, were listening.

Anne decided she wouldn't give them that satisfaction. "Nothing's wrong." She smiled up at him. "Except that I'm a little cold."

"Let's go inside and warm up." His response was automatic. She knew that although she might be fooling the others, the kids who'd known her all her life, she wasn't fooling Jay.

"I'm cold too," Clarisa called. "Let's run."

They raced madly toward the stone ranch house and

arrived puffing at the great front door. Only Jay didn't seem to be out of breath.

Steve, a pleasant, rather heavyset boy from band who was Clarisa's date, looked at the taller boy. "You must be in good shape," he commented with a grin. "You aren't gasping for breath like the rest of us."

Anne was reminded of the fight at school. She'd never gotten a chance to ask him about that. "Yeah," she said. "How come you managed to land Rod on the floor like that when he's so much bigger than you?"

She supposed he hadn't landed too many people on the floor lately. He looked embarrassed. "Until a year ago my dad kept our apartment in the neighborhood where he'd grown up. He said he didn't want to forget his roots."

Anne frowned questioningly. "What does that have to do with your being in good shape?"

"It's an inner-city neighborhood," Jay explained. "People are close-knit in some ways, they have to be, but you have to be able to stand up for yourself, too. And I go to gym regularly and work out."

"I guess you moved away when your dad got sick," Anne said, trying to piece together the picture of Jay's past. She'd had it wrong. She'd pictured him as growing up in some well-manicured urban community. But it hadn't been like that at all. "He must have wanted things different when he started having his heart problem."

Jay shook his head. "I almost think that's where the problem started. Mom and Dad grew up in that neighborhood. It was old, but not really rundown. It was hard on Dad when we had to move. He said it was like the past had vanished and he wasn't sure there was any future."

Abruptly Jay looked around as if suddenly aware of where he was. But even Clarisa didn't look like she wanted to make fun of him.

Jay was making progress with her friends by being himself. Too bad the two of them weren't getting along as well.

"Why did you move from the old neighborhood," Clarisa asked, "if your father felt that way about it? Were you the one who wanted to move?"

"Not me." Jay shook his head. "But the city decided

the area needed to be redone. A whole block of apartments was torn down."

"Oh." Clarisa thought about that for a moment. "What did they build to replace them?"

"A parking lot." Jay's answer was brief and bitter.

"So you don't belong anyplace now?" Anne couldn't help asking.

"We have an apartment, but it's not like home."

She nodded. This helped her to understand him better. She thought of the old-fashioned house on the hill in Bryan. Most of her life she'd been planning what things would be like when she moved away from it, but she didn't want it to stop existing. She liked the idea of that house being there so she could come back and take a look at it anytime she wanted to.

"Party's getting dull." Jay looked around at the three of them with a grin. "Guess that's my fault."

Anne didn't say that it was the first time she'd seen him relax around her friends. "We'll forgive you this time," she said instead.

He looked at her questioningly, as though trying to figure out whether she really meant it or was playing games with him again.

But there was no more time to talk. They went on into the crowded den of the ranch house, warming themselves at the big log fire, then chatting politely with Mr. and Mrs. Michaels.

For the hundredth time Anne couldn't help being amazed that Susan Michaels could have perfectly normal, rather pleasant parents.

"Food in the kitchen," Mrs. Michaels said. Obediently they drifted in that direction.

They heaped paper plates with hamburgers, baked beans, chips, and pickles, and took cups of hot chocolate.

"Let's go back out on the porch to eat," Steve suggested, looking around at the elbow-to-elbow crowd.

"Good idea," Jay echoed enthusiastically. "If the girls don't think it's too cold." He looked questioningly at Anne.

It was hard to remember why she'd been so mad at him. She'd never been this way before. Always in the past, she'd been the levelheaded member of the Hollis clan. And now she was going up and down emotionally so fast it practically made her head spin.

Was this what being in love was like?

8

Outside, the night was clear and cold and stars sparkled distantly. Nothing was changed except that Anne wasn't mad at Jay anymore.

Her own swiftly changing feelings were a mystery to her. When the foursome sat on the steps of the stone porch to eat their food, Anne discovered one piece of information. Being in love didn't lessen her appetite.

When the last morsel of food was gone, Steve got to his feet. "Clarisa and I need to get back to town," he said. "How about meeting us at Ryerson's for a snack later?"

"How can you talk about food," Clarisa asked with a groan, "considering how much you've just eaten?"

"A mere appetizer, my dear." Steve grinned, showing a flash of teeth in the darkness. He turned back to Jay and Anne. "How about it?"

Jay looked at Anne. "It's okay with me," she said.

"We'll meet you," he told Steve and Clarisa.

Anne and Jay stood together, watching the small blond girl and the big, dark-haired boy walk away.

"Steve's nice," Anne commented. "He and Clarisa are both so interested in music. But she's known him all her life, and she takes him for granted."

She felt Jay's eyes on her. "Maybe we should go back inside," she commented nervously. Because it was so cold, they were alone on the porch. Most of the sophomores were inside the ranch house eating now.

He moved nearer to her and she wondered once again if he was going to kiss her. "Do you want to go back inside?"

She shook her head. "No, but I suppose we'd better go

in and say good night to Susan's parents and the other sponsors."

"Okay." He didn't move. "Why did you get so mad at me before?"

She didn't deny her anger, but tried to think how to explain it. It was hard to say that the world had seemed wrapped in a rosy balloon and he'd reached out with his words to puncture it.

"I *do* believe in love at first sight," she said stubbornly, not looking at him. "My mom and dad fell in love that way. They told me so."

He took that in silently.

"Dad said he took one look at Mom and that's all there was to it. He knew he wanted to spend the rest of his life with her."

"It doesn't always happen that way." He sounded like he was discussing a math problem, not something that had to do with them personally. "And your dad could have found out the next time he saw her that he couldn't stand your mom."

"He didn't," Anne snapped.

He stepped away from her. "Let's go in and get the good nights over."

How could boys be so unromantic!

They went inside and said their thank-yous and good-byes, then drove back to town, exchanging no more than a couple of sentences during the drive. At Ryerson's the presence of Clarisa and Steve loosened things up a bit, but later, when they stood in front of Anne's house, words failed them once again.

Anne could smell the fading scent of the frosted roses, like the dried petals Mom scattered through the drawers of her chest. It was getting colder rapidly and she huddled deeper in her jacket.

Jay stood with both hands stuffed in his pockets, staring down at her, but she couldn't discern his expression in the darkness.

"I had a good time," he said.

"I did too."

"Thanks for inviting me."

"Sure." Somehow this conversation wasn't going at all

the way love scenes did in the movies. Maybe this wasn't being in love at all!

She turned to climb the porch steps and go inside.

"Anne." His voice was suddenly urgent.

She turned to face him. Standing on the second step, she was nearer to his height.

His voice was nearly a whisper. "I don't believe in love at first sight," he said, "but it seems to have happened to me in spite of that."

Anne stared at him in the darkness a moment longer, then reached up to gently touch her face against his jaw.

"It's something that's hard to believe until it happens to you," she admitted.

But he wasn't through yet. "And it was still there at the second meeting, and the next. I guess it'll go on and on for the rest of my life."

Anne moved back a step, disconcerted by the sudden seriousness in his tone. Instinctively she knew she wasn't ready for this.

He reached for her, pulling her gently into his arms. He hesitated a moment before he kissed her.

Anne felt her lips tremble.

Then he smiled at her. "Your sisters will be worried. Go on inside."

She was conscious of him standing there watching her as she unlocked the front door and went inside. She tip-toed through the house and up the stairs, hearing them creak under her feet in the darkness. She expected Nikki to call out and say something about her coming home late. But nothing happened.

The bathroom light cast a dim glow down the upstairs hall. Hurriedly Anne brushed her teeth and put on pajamas. By the time she got into bed, she was shivering in the unheated house and the covers felt warm and comforting.

She planned to think of Jay and the evening she'd just lived through, but fell almost immediately into exhausted sleep and didn't wake until morning.

She was awakened by a shriek. She sat up in bed abruptly. "What's wrong?" she called out.

"Look at this!" Leslie was at Anne's window, staring down on the front lawn.

Anne scowled sleepily at her sister. "What are you doing in my room?" she growled.

"I was going down the hall when I glanced across to your window and thought I saw something," Leslie explained in an amused voice. "And was I right!"

Anne knew Leslie was baiting her. Se refused to bite. "Go away," she mumbled, pulling the covers up over her head. "It's Saturday morning and I can sleep late."

"If you know what's good for you, you'd better come and take a look," Leslie advised darkly. "You'll want to see this before Nikki does."

Anne lowered the covers enough to peer out. "See what?" she asked suspiciously.

Leslie turned to look wickedly at her. "Nikki's going to be so upset."

Anne didn't want to show that she was getting concerned, so she climbed slowly from the bed, wincing as her bare feet touched the cold floor. "I can see right now you're not going to give me any peace until I do what you want," she grumbled, "but this better be good, Leslie Hollis, to wake me on Saturday morning!"

She hurried across the floor to the big double window. What she saw made her gasp with surprise.

"Didn't I tell you?" Leslie gloated. "I've seen houses rolled before, but this must be the all-time masterpiece."

"Oh . . . my . . ." was all Anne could say. Leslie was right. She'd never seen anything quite like this.

The huge old trees in the Hollis yard, the many bushes and shrubs had served as the perfect setting for last night's exterior decorators.

Rolls of bathroom tissue had been tossed among the trees in such a fashion that they'd spun long webs of trailing white paper round and round among the branches like tinsel rope on a Christmas tree. Loose pieces of paper blew across the lawn, collecting in the damp, frosty grass, and shorter bushes and trees had been carefully draped with the long, stringy paper. The wind was getting up again and tissue paper was being blown into neighboring yards.

"We're littering the whole neighborhood," Anne exclaimed in dismay. "You'd better get right down and start gathering that stuff up before somebody complains."

"*I'd* better gather it up!" Leslie exclaimed. "Why should I have to do it? I didn't put it there."

"Your friends did it," Anne told her. "You know they did."

"It could have been your friends, or Nikki's." Leslie stepped back defiantly. "I don't see why you have to lay this dirty work at my door."

"You know very well this is the kind of thing they pull on popular kids at school," Anne told her sister. "And Nikki's not there now. I can't see college kids doing something this childish."

"Why not? Some of them aren't all that mature!"

"You should know," Anne said. "You date enough immature college men, like Eric."

"Leave Eric out of this. You have enough problems with your own social life."

"Girls!" Nikki's voice sounded from behind them and they turned to see the sleepy dark-haired girl yawning in the doorway to Anne's room. "What's going on here? You woke me from the best dream."

Just the sight of her sister was enough to remind Anne of the nasty trick Nikki had played on her about Jay. Angrily she turned back to the window, waving one hand in a sweeping gesture. "Such is the price of popularity," she said, indicating the scene below.

Nikki flopped across the room in her bedroom slippers, frowning silently on the littered yard. "What next?" she finally asked.

"Anne thinks my friends did it," Leslie said in lofty tones, "but I say there's no evidence."

Nikki regarded her with cynicism. "It doesn't matter," she said. "I know who's going to have to clean it up."

Leslie propped her elbows on the windowsill. "I had plans for this morning," she said. "Eric was going to take me out for breakfast and then for a drive."

"It'll have to be lunch," Nikki advised her sister grimly. "Right, Anne?"

Anne didn't look at Nikki. It would be a long, long time

before she would forgive her sister. She'd thought Nikki was to be trusted. "Whatever you say," she answered icily.

She could almost feel Nikki's reaction to her tone. "I was trying to do what I thought best, Annie."

Anne couldn't answer.

"What's going on?" Leslie questioned.

Neither of them answered her. Finally Anne made dismissing gestures with her hands. "If you want me to help clean up, then get out of here so I can get dressed."

"We'd all better get dressed." Nikki sounded relieved to change the subject.

"Can't we eat first?" Leslie asked. How like her middle sister that was, Anne thought, amused despite her dismay at the condition of the yard. If her breakfast drive was spoiled, Leslie would make sure she ate anyway!

"Better not." Nikki shook her head. "We don't want that stuff blowing all over the neighborhood."

Anne dressed hurriedly in her warmest clothing, then pulled on a downy ski jacket and a warm knit cap. It looked cold outside.

She was the first one out of the house and she stood surveying the yard at closer range. Then she saw the old clunker family car sitting in the driveway. It had been elaborately decorated, apparently with white shoe polish.

She ran over to look more closely at it. The window in front of the driver's seat was neatly covered with a block of white, making visibility impossible; graffiti decorated the rest of the windows and the body of the car itself. Anne circled the automobile, reading inoffensive, but hardly funny messages; but the words drawn across the broad back window stopped her cold.

It was like a grade-school drawing made on a sidewalk. Inside a roughly drawn valentine of a heart were the words, "Anne and Jay"!

She stared numbly at it. Suddenly the whole incident changed shape in her mind.

Before, when she thought it something done by Leslie's friends, it had seemed only mildly irritating, almost funny. Popular kids got this kind of treatment.

But she was Anne, and though she had her own

friends, she wasn't particularly well-known at school, and no one could accuse her of being wildly popular.

She was still staring numbly at the automobile when her sisters came up behind her.

"Oh, no," Nikki moaned. "And I've got to drive to Fort Davis today to do research for my paper on the Indian Wars."

"Indian Wars?" Leslie's voice came through Anne's brain only dimly. "That's the first I've heard of it."

"I've mentioned it a hundred times," Nikki answered indignantly. "It's for that correspondence history course I took this summer. I'm just finishing up the work."

"You're always studying," Leslie returned. "I don't pay any attention to that."

"I heard her say something about it," Anne admitted.

"You'll have to clean up the car while Anne and I work on the yard, Leslie," Nikki ordered.

"I'll clean it up," Anne offered. "It's my fault."

She heard surprised exclamations from behind her, but didn't turn around. Instead, she led them to the back of the car and pointed to the valentine-decorated rear window. "You were right, Nikki," she admitted. "It's because everybody thought it was disloyal for me to date Jay. This wasn't just for fun. This was a dirty, mean trick!"

"Oh, no, honey, I don't think so." Nikki's protest came in a shocked rush. Anne felt her sister's hand touch her shoulder, and she pulled away.

"You should understand." She spat out the words furiously. "You deliberately kept Jay's message from me. You were trying to break us up."

Anne couldn't face her oldest sister. "I'll go get some rags and soapy water," she called, already running toward the house. "I'll get the car ready for you to use."

"Wait, Anne!" Nikki sounded hurt, but Anne didn't care. It was time somebody realized the kind of damage the youngest member of the family was enduring.

When she came out with the necessary supplies for cleaning the car, Nikki and Leslie were busily at work cleaning up the lawn.

"Nikki didn't mean to cause trouble," Leslie yelled. Obviously the two girls had been talking.

Anne ignored her. Instead, she turned on the hose and began washing the car.

Nikki didn't say anything, but Leslie kept up a shouted monologue, aimed at Anne. Anne pretended she couldn't hear.

She bent her head and concentrated on scrubbing the car. The cold wind chilled her wet hands, but she ignored that too, scrubbing until the front window was covered with a white paste of mixed shoe polish and sudsy water.

"You're really mean, Anne," Leslie shouted. "Nikki looks like she's ready to cry."

"I am not!" Nikki shouted angrily.

"She knocks herself out for you, spoils you rotten, always has since you were a little girl, and this is the way you repay her."

Anne determinedly shut her middle sister's strident voice out of her mind.

None of them was accomplishing much, Anne noticed when she looked around. Leslie stood in one place, clutching a wadded mass of tissue. Nikki was collecting paper from the shrubs in front of the house.

"Mind your own business," Anne shouted furiously at her sister.

"You might at least pay attention to what I'm saying," Leslie returned icily.

Anne turned her back, scrubbing even harder.

She didn't know who she was maddest at: Nikki and Leslie, or the kids who'd rolled the house and painted the car.

"Nikki was only trying to look after you. She was afraid of what people would think about you dating Jay."

"You didn't consider other people's opinions important," Anne pointed out calmly, not turning around.

"I felt it was a good idea for you to see him," Leslie admitted, her voice moderating slightly.

Anne didn't say anything.

"What harm could it do?" Leslie went on. "He's the son of Dad's boss and it was a chance for you to put in a good word for us. What did it cost you but a little time. And it could very well have saved the day for Dad."

Anne's mouth tightened. How could Leslie think she

would do such a thing? She'd show them all, everybody who'd misunderstood, and particularly the ones who'd made this mess of the Hollis' front yard. She'd show them she could go on acting as she wished, as she thought right . . . even if nobody agreed with her, even if she had to walk alone.

She was suddenly aware of a stricken silence behind her. "What's wrong, Leslie?" she asked, turning around, a wet rag uplifted in a solidly chilled hand. "Cat got your—"

She saw the figure of a tall boy, his red hair covered by a winter cap, standing at the edge of the lawn staring at her. From her sisters' frozen faces she knew they'd seen him at least a full moment before she had.

"Jay!" she said, glad to see him, glad to have this one bright moment in a totally dreary day.

He stared at her a moment longer before speaking. His face was white with shock.

"Is that why?" His voice came out a hoarse croak, as though he had a sore throat.

Anne stared at him, not understanding, then looked to her sister.

"We didn't see him coming." Leslie apologized in a whisper that was nearly lost in the wind. "He heard what we said."

"What we said?" Anne asked puzzled. It seemed to her that nobody had been talking but Leslie.

"Is that why you've been dating me?" Jay asked, his voice no more normal than it had been before. "What Leslie said . . . is that the way it was?"

Anne tried to remember what Leslie had said last: that nonsense about dating Jay to help Dad . . .

"Oh!" She realized an instant later that she'd said the word aloud.

"We'd better go inside, Leslie." Nikki moved swiftly, tugging at her sister's arm. "I'm chilled absolutely to the bone, and I need some hot chocolate."

For once Leslie was agreeable. "Oh, sure." She thrust the paper she was holding into a trash can. "I'm with you. Hot chocolate sounds great."

Neither Anne nor Jay said anything until the door

closed behind the two girls. Then, his face set in stern lines, Jay advanced slowly toward her.

He can't believe it, Anne assured herself. He has to know me better than that.

He looked incredibly hurt. "I don't know what you thought I had to do with your dad's work."

"I didn't. It was Leslie, and other people. They said you were here to check on Dad and maybe have him replaced."

"That's why you went out with me, pretended we were friends?"

"Yes. I mean, no. Of course not! I didn't even know who you were that first time we met. It was after that I heard the talk and everyone started telling me I should go out with you or I shouldn't go out with you. Leslie was one of the shoulds." She tried to explain logically, but had the feeling it wasn't coming out clear at all.

A light rain started to fall, whipped by wind, dashing across her face like windblown tears. She was cold, so cold she could hardly think.

For the first time Jay seemed to see the car and the yard. "What happened here?" he asked, sounding more like himself for the first time.

Anne showed him the half-intact heart.

"I can't make out the words," he said, bending closer. "They're smeared."

"I was trying to wash it off. It said Anne and Jay, inside a big heart like a kindergarten kid would draw."

He looked at her as though his eyes could see straight through into her mind. "You didn't like that. You didn't like having somebody write that you love me."

"It's not that," Anne protested. "But it was a mean joke. Anyway, Nikki needs the car and she can't drive it with it looking this way." A thought occurred to her. "Where's your car?"

"Dad has it. He wanted to go down to the store and I didn't think it would be a good idea for him to walk in this weather. So I thought I'd come over and see if we could go for a stroll. I guess it was a good thing I did." He reached down for a sodden piece of paper, placing it as carefully in the trash can as though it was an object of value. "Otherwise I'd never have known what the score was. I would have gone on thinking you liked me."

"But I do," Anne protested, sounding feeble against his bitterness. "And friends trust each other."

"Friends!" he returned the word bleakly.

She didn't know what to say. What words were there to convince him the plan Leslie had been talking about was her own, not Anne's? What was the use anyway of trying to convince him, if he was willing to believe such a thing of her?

He was halfway across the yard before he turned around. "My dad sent me here because he's trying to get me interested in his business," he told her. "He wanted me to look over one of the stores and get an idea how it's run. But I wouldn't interfere with his employees, not even if he'd let me."

He walked away then. Anne watched him go, feeling as bitter and cold inside as the wintry day. Finally, when he was out of sight, she went inside.

Leslie and Nikki were waiting in the living room. They'd been talking about her, she knew by the way the conversation suddenly stopped when she came into the house.

"I hope you're satisfied," she told them.

The angry words were somehow remote from her. Tomorrow she would cry and feel awful about Jay, but right now she only felt empty. Empty, and so cold she'd probably never be warm again.

She went over to stand next to the wall furnace.

"Your poor hands are red," Nikki said, hurrying to her side. She touched Anne's hand with the tip of a finger. "You're practically frozen from washing the car in that cold wind."

Anne pulled away, turning her back to her sister. She wasn't in the mood for any of Nikki's big-sister airs. "I'll go back out and finish in a minute so you can go on your trip."

"She probably won't go anyway," Leslie interjected hurriedly, "not now that it's raining."

Nikki walked over to stare out at the miserable day. "I

wish I could call it off, but the paper is due Monday and I've got to have this last bit of information."

"Then get Mike to drive with you," Leslie urged.

"Can't. He's out of town."

It might have seemed funny at some other time, the way the two girls were reversing roles with Leslie looking after Nikki for a change. But nothing was very funny today.

Anne told herself she would never forgive either of her sisters for the part they'd played in bringing that look of deep hurt to Jay's face.

Let Nikki solve her own problems. Anne didn't care if she got the first failing mark of her life on the Indian paper.

"We'll get the car cleaned up," Leslie assured her sister.

"It's no use," Nikki answered. "It's too cold to be outside washing a car. I can't have both of you getting sick just because of a paper I need to do."

Anne didn't bother to disagree.

Leslie started to say something else but was interrupted by a knock at the front door. The other two girls made no move, but Anne's heart beat faster. Maybe it was Jay, come back to tell her he'd thought the whole thing over and knew she hadn't been pretending with him.

She hurried to the door and flung it open, allowing a smattering of rain into the living room. Her heart dropped with a thud at the sight of the handsome young man standing there.

He smiled, flashing television-commerical white teeth. In fact, everything about Eric Luton's appearance was that of a handsome leading man.

"Anne. Is Leslie here?"

"I'm here." Leslie spoke from deep in the living room. For the first time Anne realized they hadn't turned on the lights. The dreary day outside did little to cheer the gloomy interior.

Eric shaded his eyes with his hand as though trying to see at some great distance. "Leslie Hollis?" he called. "Are you somewhere inside this deep cave?"

It was another quality about Eric that Anne didn't admire: his tendency to be cute. She couldn't understand what Leslie saw in him.

But then, tastes were different. Nikki's Mike was too bookish. Only Jay was just right; and nobody else—not Nikki, Leslie, or even Clarisa—agreed with that judgment. He was right only for Anne.

She felt sick to her stomach at the thought of him. Was this part of being in love too: caring so much it made you ill?

"I'm here, Eric," Leslie finally responded.

"Looks like you girls had visitors last night." His voice was so cheerful it made Anne's head ache.

"What do you mean?" Leslie asked, coming into view. Then her expression cleared. "You're talking about the yard."

He nodded, then looked more closely at Leslie. "Don't look so upset, Les. It's just a little prank by your friends."

"Not my friends," Leslie retorted.

"Not my friends either," Anne slashed. "More like my enemies." She wished she was old enough to pack up right this minute and move away from Bryan.

Eric edged his athletic body toward the door as if uncertain what he'd stepped into. "Ready to go, Les?" he urged.

"I have to help Anne clean up the yard first. Maybe you'd better come back for me a little later."

"I'd be glad to help," he offered, still cheerful.

Anne knew she couldn't take a whole morning of Eric. "I'd rather do it myself," she said. "You two go on for your breakfast and drive." For the first time that day she looked directly at Nikki. "And you go on over to the old fort and do your research."

"I hate for you to go alone," Leslie said to Nikki, "in such bad weather."

Anne couldn't decide if it was a deliberate hint or not, but Eric picked it up immediately. "If Nikki needs to go over to Fort Davis, we can drive her," he told Leslie.

Nikki blushed a delicate pink. "That's not necessary," she protested primly.

"It is necessary," Leslie insisted. "There's no way you can drive our car. Anyway, Eric doesn't mind."

"You know I'd be happy to help your sister," Eric smiled benevolently.

It was sickening. Anne decided to ignore the whole conversation. She didn't care what they did. Instead, she walked over to the hall closet and began searching through an accumulation of debris on the shelf for some of the winter gloves they had put away last spring. Finally she found a pair of leather ones, lined in warm fur, and pulled them on. They felt terrific on her only slightly thawed hands.

"But we can't leave without helping Anne clean up the yard," Nikki protested.

"You sure can," Anne informed her. "I'd rather do it myself than listen to the two of you. So get going."

"But Anne!" The protest was Leslie's.

"I'll be fine, Leslie," Anne said. "But you'd better get going before the weather gets worse."

"All right," Leslie said finally. "We should be back around noon."

The four of them went out of the house together, but Anne went no farther than the front lawn while Nikki, Leslie, and Eric climbed into the front seat of his convertible. Even with the top up, Anne thought it looked as if it would be cold inside the car. Convertibles were just right when the sun was shining and the weather warm. But on a day like this, they looked like tropical beasts that had strayed too far north.

The car wheeled sharply away from the curb, skidding on the slick surface of the street. Anne grinned. Nikki was going to have a miserable drive hanging on to the edge of her seat. She'd always hated fast driving.

9

Anne didn't make another attempt to clean up the car, but within a couple of hours she'd done all she could do to clear the yard.

She looked up into the tall cedar, one of the tallest trees in town, and sighed. No way could she climb high enough to get those wisps of paper blown into the skinny branches at the very top. Well, she'd done the best she could, and it was getting so cold that even the warm clothing she was wearing was inadequate against the sharpness of the wind.

Nikki and Leslie should be home soon, anyway. She wanted a chance to clean up, eat, and retreat to her room before they barged back in telling her what to do.

Instead of showering, she lit the bathroom heater and luxuriated in a long, very hot bath. Afterward she put on a thick terry-cloth robe and fuzzy slippers and went back downstairs.

She glanced at the clock. It was nearly noon and she'd had nothing to eat. Maybe that was why she felt so awful inside.

She opened a can of vegetable soup and heated it, then placed a large bowl, a packet of saltines, and a glass of milk on a tray. She took the food up to her room. She would eat there so Nikki and Leslie couldn't barge in on her privacy.

But by the time the bowl was empty, they still hadn't come back. She walked over to the window, frowning at the bleak day outside. It looked more like November than September.

The phone rang. It was Mom and Dad, still enthusiastically enjoying their holiday, and Anne had to pretend

nothing was wrong. Apparently she was convincing, because they didn't ask what was bothering her, accepting
her explanation for Nikki's and Leslie's absence without
question.

"Eric drove them over to the old fort," she explained.
"Nikki had to do some research for a paper."

"Nikki went in Eric's car?" Anne could almost feel the
upraised eyebrows in Mom's voice. "The way she's always
complained about his driving?"

"I guess she changed her mind." Anne didn't mention
the bad weather or the changed appearance of their own
car. "It must be lovely and warm in California," she commented, trying not to sound wistful as she thought of the
blustery day outside.

"It's warm and summery," Mom enthused. "I'm trying
to get a tan because I know in our part of the country
we'll be seeing some bad weather soon."

"Soon." Anne echoed the word brightly.

They said good-bye without suspecting their youngest
daughter's gloom. Anne went upstairs and changed into
some comfortable jeans and an old shirt, then picked out
a book to read.

She had to have something to do. She couldn't just sit
and think about how awful everything was.

But she found herself listening for Leslie and Nikki to
come home. The hours crept slowly by.

Nikki and Leslie had some nerve, to leave her alone all
afternoon when they knew she was so crushed about Jay.
She'd expected better of Nikki at least.

It was nearly three o'clock when she thought she heard
the sound of a car and went to look out the window. It
wasn't Eric's car, but she saw that the rain was changing,
beginning to freeze into a thin sheet on the streets.

An image of the roads between Bryan and Fort Davis
flashed into her mind . . . winding, wet, mountainous
roads. She shook her head. Leslie was right. She was getting to be a worrier like Nikki.

But they were hours late!

She began to pace the floor in front of the large window that looked out onto the street in front of the house,
watching for the first sign of Eric's car.

If they'd been delayed, they could at least have called.

She wondered if this was how Nikki had felt when she, Anne, was late. But she'd never been this late! Leslie had said they would be back by noon and here it was the middle of the afternoon.

That car of Eric's was his pride and joy; he took terrific care of it. But any car could suffer an unexpected breakdown. Probably they were stranded at some garage, awaiting repairs, right now.

No, that couldn't be it. The garage would have a phone and Nikki would have remembered to call her.

She revised the mental picture. The breakdown must have occurred out on the road someplace. Traffic wasn't heavy on the fort road even in good weather. They might have to wait for quite a while before getting help.

She felt a little better at the thought. It would serve Nikki and Leslie right when they came dragging in here and Anne got a chance to scold them for being late.

She tried to hold on to the picture. Resolutely she refused to let anything worse cross her mind.

It wasn't easy, though. She went into the kitchen, peering restlessly through the shelves for some delectable nibble, but nothing looked very good. A blaring emergency siren only a few blocks away did nothing to increase her appetite.

She was getting so mad at Nikki and Leslie . . . Eric, too. They had no business worrying her this way.

The sudden ringing of the doorbell jolted her. Then she relaxed, grinning. They were home and she would be so glad to see them she wasn't even sure she'd be able to stay mad. She tried to put on a frown as she walked leisurely across the kitchen. Let 'em wait!

But her relief had faded before she even got out of the room. Nikki and Leslie each had house keys. They wouldn't ring the doorbell.

Unless they were too cold and tired to fumble around in a purse looking for a key. She ran to the front door.

She'd never thought to be disappointed at the sight of Jay. "It's only you," she said, sagging limply against the door.

His face was white, his expression disturbed.

"I don't feel like arguing anymore," she told him.

"Let me come in, Anne."

She frowned as he brushed past her.

"I said I would tell you." He turned protectively toward her. "I couldn't let you hear by phone . . . or some other way. I made them let me be the one."

A chill that had nothing to do with the open door crept about her. She tried to take in what he was saying. "Tell me what?"

He placed a hand on each of her shoulders. "It may not be so bad. Sometimes these things look worse than they are."

Anne tried to smile, but her lips felt stiff. "I don't know what you're talking about."

He guided her over to the sofa and made her sit down. She felt like exploding. "I know you're trying to break something gently, but you're only making it worse. Please just come out and say whatever it is."

Before he could answer, the sound of running footsteps reached them and Clarisa poked her troubled face through the open doorway.

She looked at Jay. "Have you told her?"

He didn't answer, but turned back to Anne. "I was down at Ryerson's having a shake when I heard. One of the ambulance drivers had come by there after it happened. Your sisters were in an accident."

"They're both hurt," Clarisa added in a sober tone.

"But not badly," Jay added quickly.

Anne found her voice with difficulty. Her throat felt dry. "How do you know?"

"About the accident? I told you."

"Not that, but that they weren't badly hurt?"

When he didn't answer, she knew he didn't know but was only trying to help her feel better.

"Maybe it's a mistake," Anne decided. "A car like Eric's was in an accident and everyone jumped to the wrong conclusion."

"Anne." Clarisa touched her hand. "Eric just called from the hospital. He said Mom and I should come over and tell you. I ran so I got here first, but she's coming right behind me."

Mrs. Madison's appearance at the front door at that very moment confirmed Anne's fears. It was true.

"I have my car out front," Jay assured her.

The usually outspoken Mrs. Madison didn't say anything until after the three young people were outside and she had carefully closed the door behind them.

"Clarisa and I will run and get our car," she said. "We'll meet you at the hospital."

Anne's brain seemed set on automatic. She heard her own voice calmly directing Jay to the nearby hospital.

"It's only a little hospital," she told him as they got out of the Corvette, "but we have good doctors."

He patted her shoulder comfortingly.

"It was my fault they went," she said as they walked toward the emergency entrance. "If our car hadn't been messed up, they would have taken it and not even been in Eric's car."

"No good thinking that way," he told her.

He was right. The trick of getting through this was not to think at all. She tried to make her mind a blank, but it wasn't easy. She kept seeing crashing cars.

She recognized the boy standing down the hall. "Eric!" She broke into a run. "Eric. Tell me how they are."

He stepped back, looking confused. "Nobody's told me yet."

"What happened?" Jay asked, putting the warm pressure of his arm around Anne.

Suddenly Anne realized the two boys hadn't met. "This is Jay Ogden," she said, polite as a little girl at a make-believe tea party. "This is Eric Luton, Jay."

"It wasn't my fault, Anne," Eric said, speaking in a high, excited voice. "I might have been going a little fast, but it made me nervous the way Nikki kept asking me to slow down. Anybody could have had trouble on that curve with the roads as slick as they are."

Anne didn't speak.

"You failed to make a curve?" Jay asked.

"The one just outside of town. We'd been a long time over at the fort, listening to some old guy tell Nikki all sorts of boring stuff, and I was trying to hurry so Les and I would have time for some fun, and . . . and we skidded.

The car went flying onto the shoulder. I tried to get control, but we went into a utility pole."

Anne could hear the sound of her own breathing.

"It wasn't my fault," Eric said again.

"Tell us how the girls were," Jay said. "How were they when they came in here?"

Eric didn't speak for a moment. "I didn't come in with them. They brought me in a police car. Right after the wreck Nikki was crumpled up kind of funny in the backseat, but she talked to me. She seemed all right."

"And Leslie?" Anne asked.

"She was thrown against the windshield." Anne's anger was lessened by the pain in his voice. He really did care about Leslie. "She was out cold. She didn't even wake up when they lifted her onto a stretcher."

Anne drew a deep, shaky breath.

"Anne!" Clarisa ran up to them and Anne could see Mrs. Madison coming down the hall. "Did you find out anything?"

"Not much." Anne shook her head.

Mrs. Madison bustled up to them. "Any word?"

"Not yet," her daughter answered.

Mrs. Madison took charge. She made Anne sit down in the waiting room, sent Clarisa for coffee and sandwiches. Anne couldn't eat a bite, but to please her friend's mother she sipped at black, bitter-tasting coffee.

Waiting was the worst thing in the world.

"Anne, shall I call your parents?" Mrs. Madison asked.

Anne looked around at her friends. She started to ask them what she should do, but the words froze on her tongue. This situation involved her sisters, her mother, and her father. She knew them better than anyone else. It was her decision to make.

Jay squeezed her hand. "They could get on a plane and be back here in no time."

Anne shook her head. "Wait," she said. "Once the doctors tell us what the situation is, then we'll call them. There's no use putting them through unnecessary worry."

Mrs. Madison nodded agreement. "We should hear something any minute."

It seemed much longer than a minute to Anne; the time

stretched to a length that could be counted only in centuries. But finally she saw the familiar face of a doctor whom she'd known since childhood.

The kind-faced woman smiled at Anne, but her eyes looked grave.

"Are they going to be all right?" Anne blurted out nervously, gripping Jay's hand.

"Nikki's left leg is fractured and she has a couple of damaged ribs." The doctor smiled. "But broken bones heal."

Anne was conscious only of the fact that one sister had not yet been mentioned.

"What about Leslie?" She heard Eric's anxious voice.

The doctor hesitated for a moment. "Leslie's still unconscious."

"But it's been such a long time." Again it was Eric who spoke.

"Not so long." The doctor tried to sound comforting.

"Do you think it's serious?" Anne asked, her voice sounding so much calmer than she felt.

Again Anne sensed the slightest hesitation from the doctor before she gave her answer. "It's too early to say, Anne."

"But it could be?"

The doctor gave a reluctant nod. "She was struck on the head when she was thrown against the windshield. Our tests are inconclusive at this point, but the fact that she hasn't regained consciousness . . ." She left the sentence unfinished.

"Can I see them?" Anne asked.

"You can see Nikki. But not Leslie, not just yet."

Anne looked around at her friends. Clarisa and her mother showed identical expressions of concern. Jay's eyes were on her face. Eric was staring down the long hall as if hoping Leslie might walk down it at any minute.

Anne followed a white-clad nurse down the hall.

"It might be best not to detail the extent of Leslie's injuries to Nikki," the nurse, who was a friend of her mother's, advised. "She's had medication for pain so you'll find her a little sleepy and, perhaps, confused."

Anne tapped lightly at the door indicated, then pushed it open.

"Anne!" Nikki's smile was bright as ever and for an instant Anne was tempted to rush to her oldest sister's side and throw all her worries on the dependable shoulders she'd trusted since she was a little girl.

But then she saw that Nikki's smile was a bit wobbly, her eyes too large.

"Come here, little sister." Nikki patted the bed at her side. "Were you worried about us?" She didn't even give Anne a chance to reply. "They won't listen to me in this hospital." Her voice was slurred by the medication. "I keep telling them, but they won't listen."

Anne patted her sister's hand as though she were a child. "Won't listen to what, Nikki?"

"I told them Leslie is going to be very bored being in the hospital and they should put us in a room together so we can keep each other company. But look at this." She pointed to the empty bed on the other side of the room. "I don't even have a roommate!"

"Maybe they'll put Leslie there later." Anne tried to sound encouraging, but she had to swallow a lump at the back of her throat.

Nikki frowned as if trying to reason something out through the fog the medication had her in. "What's wrong with Leslie?" she asked abruptly.

The direct question came unexpectedly. "She hit her head," she answered truthfully before she could think.

The frown ruffled deeper into Nikki's forehead. "That sounds bad," she said. "Or was it only a little tap?"

"A little tap?"

Nikki touched her own dark hair. "You know, just a little bump, enough to give her a headache but nothing else."

"Just a little headache," Anne echoed agreeably, remembering the nurse's words. She hated lying to Nikki, but it was obvious her sister was too heavily drugged to even understand the truth.

"That Leslie! I end up with a broken leg and all she's got is a bump. I guess that's why they didn't put her in here. She's probably not even going to have to stay in the hospital."

"Maybe not."

"One good thing anyway, she'll be able to look after you." Nikki tried to raise herself from the bed, failed, and lay back again, looking white and strained from the simple action. "Don't call Mom and Dad, Anne. This would spoil their vacation and there's not a thing they could do to help. Plenty of time for them to find out when they get back home."

She sounded almost like the normal Nikki, giving orders, taking charge. Anne smiled. "Don't worry so about everybody, Nikki."

Nikki closed her eyes, tightening her lips into a firm line. "I'm sorry, Anne."

"Sorry for what?" Anne asked, not understanding.

"I can't remember . . . exactly . . . but I did something bad to you, something about Jay. I'm sorry."

"That's okay, Nikki," Anne answered. The door opened slightly and the nurse who had shown her to the room beckoned to her.

"I've got to go now, Nikki. It's time for you to get some rest."

Nikki's eyes opened. "All right," she said, "but tell Leslie to be careful about that headache, and you be sure and eat a good dinner and lock the house tonight . . . and, and . . . She seemed to be running down.

"Yes, Nikki?"

"Tell Eric I still think he drives rotten."

Anne grinned. "I'll tell him."

The grin faded when she stepped outside the door. She walked slowly, knowing her friends would be waiting, but also knowing she had a decision to make. Nikki said not to call Mom and Dad. But Nikki didn't know about Leslie.

Mom and Dad had to be told. Instead of going on down the hall, she stopped to look for a phone and was directed to the nurse's station. "I need to call my parents," she said. "They're vacationing in California."

She was shown to a telephone. She called Information for the number of the hotel where her parents were staying, writing the number down on the pad the nurse gave her. She hardly recognized her own writing.

Then, billing it to her home phone, she placed the call. Mom and Dad responded quickly. "We'll get the first plane out," Dad assured her. "We'll be on our way to the airport within ten minutes. In the meantime, see that everything needed is done for your sisters."

"We'll be there before you know it, baby." Mom grabbed the receiver to deliver the last comforting message.

Baby! It didn't sound so bad anymore.

Jay and her friends would be wondering what had happened to her, but she needed a moment more to figure things out. She went into the room across the hall from the nurse's station. It had been fixed up as a tiny chapel.

She sank down onto one of the soft chairs. Dad had said she must see to it that the girls had what they needed.

Nikki was fine. She was well cared for. But Leslie . . .

Anne looked around, her gaze settling on a small vase of plastic flowers. This was a good hospital, with an excellent staff, but it was small and somewhat limited.

Decisively she got to her feet and went down the hall. Dr. Gardiner was back again, engaged in earnest conversation with Mrs. Madison.

"Anne!" Jay's face brightened at the sight of her. "How's Nikki?"

"Doing okay." She hadn't had time to think about Jay this afternoon; their quarrel was still unresolved, but it was good having him close like this. She took his hand, then turned to face the doctor.

Dr. Gardiner ruffled her already disturbed gray hair. She looked tired. "I've been considering calling your parents, Anne, if you'll give me the number where they can be reached. I want to talk to them about Leslie's condition."

Anne looked at her watch, then shook her head. "I already called them. They said they would be out of the hotel within ten minutes and on the way to the airport."

"Oh, dear," Mrs. Madison said. "It'll take several

hours to get here even if they do manage to get an immediate flight."

"And then the drive from the airport at Odessa. That's at least another three hours before they get here," Clarisa told her mother.

Anne kept her eyes on the doctor's face. "Mom and Dad told me to see that my sisters were looked after until they got here. I've been thinking, Doctor, that maybe . . ." She hesitated, trying to think how to word her request. She didn't want Dr. Gardiner, whom she liked and trusted, to think she considered Bryan's medical facilities less than adequate.

But people's feelings couldn't matter in this situation. It was her job to see that Leslie got the best medical care possible.

She plunged right in. "This is a small hospital. Does it have the equipment and specialists Leslie needs?"

Dr. Gardiner permitted herself a tiny smile. "I was going to explain to your parents the advisability of having her transferred by air elsewhere. She could come to consciousness at any moment, of course, but if her condition doesn't change soon I'd like to have her flown to El Paso."

Anne shook her head confusedly. "El Paso?"

The doctor nodded. "I can arrange for a helicopter staff with a medical team to take her there. But I have to go ahead and make the calls if we want them here this evening."

Anne looked at Jay and the others. Desperately she wished someone could make this decision for her. The care Leslie needed would probably be expensive and maybe not even necessary . . . maybe she should wait until Mom and Dad were here to decide. But Dr. Gardiner thought the decision should be made right now.

"Go ahead and make the arrangements," she said.

The doctor nodded and started to walk away. But Jay spoke to her retreating back. "Can Anne see Leslie?" he asked. "It would make her feel a lot better."

Anne looked gratefully at Jay. It was a request she hadn't thought to make for herself.

Dr. Gardiner thought about it. "Just for a minute," she finally said.

Jay walked her down the hall to the large room that served as an intensive-care area. He waited outside while she went in.

Leslie was the only patient, but a nurse sat by her side, keeping close attention. At first Anne almost didn't recognize her sister.

Leslie looked pale and shrunken, a golden-haired child sleeping in the narrow bed. Long lashes lay closed across an intensely white face. Tubes spread out from her slender body.

"Oh, Leslie," Anne said brokenly.

10

The nurse seemed to sense Anne's need for privacy, her wish to be alone with her sister.

"I'll step outside for an instant," she said.

Anne nodded, blinking back tears. She watched the door close behind the white figure, then looked down at her sister once again.

She'd been mad at Leslie so many times. Her sister was stubborn, sometimes self-centered, careless. But right now, Anne would have given almost anything to have Leslie open her eyes and smile.

She took hold of one of her sister's slender hands, being careful not to dislodge the tube connected to her wrist.

"I'm here, Leslie," she said. "And Mom and Dad are on their way."

Her sister didn't stir.

It was maddening. Anne wanted to shake her into wakefulness. "Leslie Hollis," she ordered sternly, "you open your eyes right now and quit scaring everyone to death!"

The long lashes didn't move. But seconds later, Leslie's lips moved slightly. "Anne?" she whispered.

Anne stared in disbelief. Dr. Gardiner had said Leslie might wake up at any moment!

Then she turned and ran to the door. "Nurse!" she yelled. "Nurse, come here."

The woman raced into the room, ignoring Anne as she dashed to her patient's side. "What's wrong?" she asked.

Jay, alarmed by Anne's call, had also come into the room, but the nurse was too intent on Leslie to notice his uninvited presence.

"She spoke to me," Anne explained.

The nurse's stiff position relaxed. "Oh, honey," she said, "I can understand how badly you want her to speak to you."

"No!" Anne stomped a foot in frustration. "She said my name. She said 'Anne.'"

The nurse gave her a pitying look. Then she saw Jay. "Perhaps you'd better take her out and get her something to eat and drink. She needs a chance to unwind a little."

Anne looked appealingly at Jay.

He stared at her for only a moment, then turned to the nurse, speaking with calm authority. "If Anne says Leslie spoke her name, then she did."

It was two against one, and though all credibility resided with the nurse, she seemed to hesitate. Then she walked over to pick up a phone. "I'll just have Dr. Gardiner paged," she said.

Anne expected they would be asked to leave at any moment, but the nurse continued to tolerate their presence, checking and rechecking Leslie's vital signs until the doctor appeared.

She looked questioningly at the three of them.

"Miss Hollis thinks her sister spoke to her," the nurse said.

"She did," Anne insisted.

An impatient look crossed the nurse's face. "If you'll step out into the hall while the doctor examines the patient," she instructed them.

But Dr. Gardiner held up a restraining hand. "It's possible." She seemed to be speaking to herself.

She looked directly at Anne. "You probably have a better chance at reaching her than the rest of us. You're her sister and something in her might have responded to your familiar voice."

Anne drew a relieved breath. It was good to be believed. "I yelled at her," she confessed. "I told her she was scaring everybody."

The doctor grinned. "I don't care if you give her a full-fledged lecture if it brings her out of this. Give it your best."

Anne looked doubtfully at the three of them. It was

one thing to talk to an unconscious Leslie when the two of them were alone together, but to do it with people watching was quite another thing.

"Go on, Anne," Jay encouraged.

She tried to shut the others out, pretending she was alone with Leslie.

"Les, you're upsetting everybody." Her voice started out wobbly, but warmed quickly. "Open your eyes and talk to me so I know you're going to be all right."

For a moment nothing happened, then something like a shudder ran along Leslie's body.

"Go on, Anne," Dr. Gardiner whispered. "Keep talking."

"Eric is worried because he feels responsible," Anne went on. "I think he's sort of fond of you. Nikki thinks you're okay. They haven't told her yet. Did you know she has a broken leg?"

Nothing happened.

"Go on, Anne," Jay told her.

"Mom and Dad are flying in, and they should be here by night." Anne halted, stopped by her sister's white face. How could this be happening? A sense of unreality gripped her. "Please wake up, Leslie?"

That frightened-child's voice of the plea seemed to reach deep into her sister's unconscious. Leslie's lashes fluttered, then opened to reveal her wide green eyes.

"Don't worry, Annie," she soothed, using Nikki's old pet name for their sister. "It'll be all right."

Dr. Gardiner stepped forward, taking immediate charge. "Leslie," she said, speaking in a clear, rather loud voice, "how do you feel?"

Leslie tried to move a hand toward her head, but couldn't because her wrist was fastened in place. "My head hurts something awful," she complained weakly. "Where's Anne? I thought I heard Anne."

Anne stepped closer once again. "I'm here, Les."

"What happened? Why am I here?"

Anne looked questioningly at the doctor. "She may not remember the accident at all," the doctor told her.

"Accident?" Leslie queried weakly.

"You and Nikki were riding with Eric and the car

skidded off the road and into a pole." Anne tried to make
the information as compact as possible.

Leslie looked as if she was having a hard time understanding. "Nikki and Eric?" she asked, wincing with the
effort of the words.

"Nikki has a broken leg, but she'll be fine. Eric didn't
get a scratch."

Leslie's lips turned up weakly. "That Eric!"

Anne and Jay were made to leave the intensive-care
area, but Anne walked away with a lighter heart.
"Hurry," she told Jay, "I want to tell the others. And I
want to get something to eat. I'm starving!"

Jay laughed. He pulled her close and touched his lips
to hers. It was a long kiss.

"Ummmm!" An elaborate throat-clearing sound
reached them and they pulled hastily apart.

Clarisa was watching them with smiling eyes. "I'm the
search party sent to find you. Mom can't understand why
you've been gone so long and Eric is having cat fits."

Anne threw her arms around her friend, dancing her
down the long hall while Jay followed with a grin on his
face.

"She's awake, Clarisa. She's awake and talking."

Anne was halfway through the hamburger Jay had
brought her before the doctor finally reappeared, but the
news was good. Leslie appeared to be on the way to
recovery and within a few hours would be placed in a
room with Nikki.

It seemed almost too good to be true. Anne only
wished there was some way of getting word to her
parents, now somewhere high in the air in a plane, and
sparing them hours of concern.

They had the long plane ride, then the three-hour drive
from the nearest airport. "Couldn't we call Odessa and
leave a message for Mom and Dad that Leslie's conscious?" she asked.

"I'll take care of it," Mrs. Madison told her. "But Clarisa's going to take you to our house and see to it that you
get some rest."

Anne knew she was too stimulated to rest, but she also

knew there was no point arguing with Mrs. Madison once she'd decided someone needed looking after.

"I'll drive them," Jay offered. He waited until Anne had finished her hamburger, then the three of them left the hospital.

It was late and very dark, but Anne didn't even mind the prickles of freezing rain that needled her face.

They were on their way to Jay's car when headlights swept up to them and a blond woman leaned her head out of a car window.

"Anne," Mrs. Turner called, "I couldn't leave the store until now, but I'm here to help you look after things." She frowned at the three of them. "Surely you're not leaving those poor injured girls here alone."

Anne didn't get a chance to speak. "Nikki and Leslie are fine," Jay said firmly, his hand on Anne's elbow.

"Anne is going to my house to rest." Clarisa's voice was equally firm. "My mother said so."

"If Mrs. Madison is in charge of things . . . I knew when I heard about the accident that you'd need someone to see everything was done right, but I couldn't leave the department unsupervised and so I was torn as to what to do." Mrs. Turner's tone was apologetic.

"Anne took care of things," Jay sounded proud.

He helped her to the car as though she was in need of guarding. After he'd dropped them off at the Madison home, with a wide grin and a quick hand squeeze for Anne, Clarisa ran water for a warm bath for Anne. Once she'd bathed and was settled in the extra bed in Clarisa's room, her friend brought her a hot drink.

Anne felt warm and safe; even the steady pelting of sleet against the bedroom window only increased her content. Only one small worry remained.

"Shouldn't Mom and Dad get here soon?" she asked.

"It'll take a while in this weather," Clarisa answered. "In fact, they may even decide to wait until morning when they get the message about how much better Leslie is."

Anne nodded. But not until Mom and Dad were back would she be able to surrender the burden of responsibility that had become hers when Leslie and Nikki were hurt. Responsibility, that was the word Nikki used too much.

"Sleep, Anne," Clarisa whispered as if from a great distance. Anne closed her eyes. She knew she'd never be able to get to sleep tonight.

When she awakened, sunlight brightened Clarisa's pretty bedroom and Mom was smiling down at her.

"Time to wake up, sleepy head," Mom said.

Anne felt like throwing her arms around her mother, but instead she grinned. "So you finally got here!"

"Finally." Mom settled on the foot of the bed. "We had to creep through sleet and wind last night."

"Leslie and Nikki okay this morning?" Anne asked, trying to sound casual.

"Both complaining and more than a little uncomfortable, but Dr. Gardiner has them in a room together so they can at least talk to each other."

"And argue," Anne added knowledgeably.

Mom smiled. "You're right about that," she said. "When I left they were debating which was worse, a concussion or a broken leg." She patted Anne's foot briskly. "Anyway, honey, Mrs. Madison has a nice hot breakfast waiting for us downstairs and your dad is anxious to see you."

Taking time only to brush her teeth and wash her face, Anne slipped back into the clothes she'd worn the night before and went downstairs with her mother. The breakfast table was a picture, with a pretty arrangement of flowers in the center and bright-yellow place mats, but Anne didn't take much time to look at it.

The best part about the room was her father's large, comforting presence. She looked from him to her mother. Surely everything would go better now.

"Hi, twirp," he greeted her, setting down a cup of hot coffee. "Aren't you going to give me a kiss?"

"Sure." Anne gave him a quick peck on the side of the face, then hugged her mother. "It's so good to have you back."

Mrs. Madison beamed on them from the kitchen door.

"Lots of pancakes and sausages coming up," she said. "Clarisa, bring in that big bottle of maple syrup."

"Clarisa up this early!" Anne exclaimed in mock surprise. "And it isn't even a school day."

"I heard that." Clarisa came into the room and put the bottle on the table. "And all I can say is, you should talk. It's nearly eleven!"

"Eleven!" Anne sank into a chair between her parents. "And I thought I was too upset to sleep."

They all laughed.

Clarisa took a bite of pancake, chewing thoughtfully before speaking. "Jay has called three times," she said casually.

"Jay?" Mom sounded interested. "Isn't that the boy you mentioned on the phone?"

"That's right," Anne admitted, conscious of the curious glances of both Clarisa and her mother.

"I told him we'd meet him at Ryerson's by noon even if I had to drag you out of bed," Clarisa went on. "He said I mustn't disturb you, that you needed your rest after yesterday, but he'd be waiting just in case."

Anne put down her fork. "I need to go back home and change clothes first."

"You've plenty of time," Mrs. Madison scolded. "Eat your breakfast first."

Anne obeyed and she had to admit that, as usual, a breakfast prepared by Mrs. Madison was the best in the world. Dad asked for a second plate of pancakes.

"I hope you enjoyed your vacation," Mrs. Madison told Anne's parents. "At least up to the time when it was cut short yesterday."

"Oh, yes," Anne's mom answered. "Dave took me to a couple of plays and we got to hear the symphony." Her eyes twinkled as she looked at her husband. "And, of course, he took advantage of the opportunity to indulge in his favorite hobby."

Dave Hollis's handsome face reddened slightly. "Now, Sue," he said.

Mrs. Hollis turned back to Mrs. Madison. "He must have visited at least a dozen stores out there just to see how they looked and get new ideas."

"Some hobby," Mrs. Madison commented with a laugh.

Sue Hollis nodded. "He's so wrapped up in Ogden's he can barely stand to take a holiday, and even when he's away he's thinking of the store half the time."

Clarisa and Anne exchanged glances. Anne knew her friend was thinking of Jay and the threat to the store.

"You manage to get fairly involved in the business yourself," Dave Hollis accused his wife. "I notice you went along with me on most of those store visits."

She laughed. "Guilty as charged."

"I'm sure everything's gone along okay while we've been away, but I thought I'd just drop by the store for a while this afternoon."

"But, Dad, you're still on vacation," Anne protested, dreading the moment when he visited the store. She was surprised that someone out at the hospital hadn't already told him about the things that had been going on. But if Dad had heard about Jay and his father, he wouldn't be feeling so cheerful.

"I might go with you," Mom said. "I want to get the girls some pretty nightgowns for their convalescence, and of course, Ogden's has the best merchandise in town."

"Of course," the rest of them chorused. Only Anne was silent.

She tried to change the subject. "What about Nikki and Leslie? Will Nikki be able to start college the way she planned?"

Mom's face sobered. "I talked to Dr. Gardiner about that. She says they'll have her fitted for crutches within a day or so, and she can enroll as scheduled on Friday. She'll need help getting around town. I told her I'd be glad to drive her, but she declined the assistance of her elderly mother. It seems Mike should be back in town in time to perform that chore."

"And Les?"

Dad answered this time. "The doctor recommends she stay out of school next week and take it easy. A head injury is nothing to take lightly.

"Does that mean no dates?" Anne asked, grinning again.

"I'm afraid so," Mom answered. "We'll probably have

to tie her to the sofa to keep her in the house. You'll have to help me keep her entertained, Anne."

"Sure," Anne agreed. For once she didn't even mind being called on to do a favor for her popular middle sister.

After breakfast, Clarisa and Anne left the adults chatting over second cups of coffee and walked over to Anne's house. She was surprised to find the outside a vastly changed world from yesterday.

The air was nippy, but the sun bright. It was sweater weather where yesterday had been full-blown overcoat time. That was just like this part of Texas: winter one day and spring the next.

"If the weather had been like this yesterday, Eric's car wouldn't have skidded," she said suddenly.

Clarisa shook her head and Anne knew what she meant. No use bothering her brain with "if onlys."

Back at the house she slipped into dark-blue pants and a matching pullover. It was a good time to wear her new boots.

They walked to the drugstore, enjoying the pleasant day and the release from the previous evening's fear.

Jay, who was seated in a booth near the back, looked up eagerly as they came in. Anne tried to smile.

Because of the accident yesterday, their misunderstanding had been set aside. But now they were back to square one and would have to start all over again.

At least he wanted to talk to her.

"Now that I've delivered you as promised, I'm going to take off," Clarisa whispered.

Anne grabbed her sleeve. "No," she whispered back, panicked. "It'll be easier if you're here."

Slowly Clarisa shook her head. "Look, Anne, I had time to talk with Jay yesterday during all the waiting. He's kind of down on himself; that's why it's hard for him to believe you really care." She waggled an admonishing finger at Anne. "Guys like that don't grow on trees, pal. Try to work it out with him."

She turned and left the drugstore, leaving Anne alone to face Jay.

"Anne!" Mr. Ryerson's voice boomed at her and it

seemed that every face in the crowded fountain area turned to look at her. "What's the latest report from the hospital?"

"Fine." Anne tried to smile, knowing the interest was genuine. But she was eager to get back to Jay and get whatever was about to happen all over with. "Nikki's going to be on crutches and Leslie's got to take it easy for a few days, but they'll be fine."

Mr. Ryerson shook his head. "I tried to tell Leslie that Luton boy was a wild driver. Why, I saw him out there one night racing down Main like it was a hot-rod strip. But she wouldn't listen. And just look what happened!" He glanced back at Jay as though to say Leslie wasn't the only one of the Hollis girls he could give advice to. "I hear your folks are back," he added meaningfully.

She made her way back through the booths of young people. She was stopped again and again to be questioned about the condition of her sisters. Finally she sat down across from Jay.

His green eyes searched her face, then he smiled. "You look a little better today."

"Did I look so awful last night?" she teased.

"Not awful." His voice was earnest. "Just exhausted and strained, like you'd been carrying the weight of the world."

That was the way it had been. She had carried the weight of the world yesterday, even if it was her own personal world.

"I used to think being grown up meant being able to decide things for yourself," she tried to explain. "You know, staying out as late as you like without having to explain to anyone, eating ice cream in bed if you feel like it. But I've finally caught on that there's more to it than that."

She didn't have to say anything else. He nodded as though he understood. She supposed he did. There was only he and his father in their little family, and his father was very ill.

"I didn't help much," he said. "I added to your problems."

Suddenly Mr. Ryerson was at the table. "Suppose you two want to order something?"

The intrusion startled Anne. She looked questioningly at Jay.

"How about your favorite," he suggested.

She shook her head. "It's a little too chilly for a shake today. How about hot chocolate with whipped cream on top?"

"Make it two," Jay told Mr. Ryerson.

Mr. Ryerson didn't depart. He looked with disapproval on Jay. "Anne's folks are back," he told the boy. "Guess Dave Hollis'll settle your hash fast enough."

"Mr. Ryerson!" Anne protested.

"I'm going. I'm going." The man edged away, still frowning his disapproval.

Anne closed her eyes, shaking her head apologetically.

"I used to think people here didn't like the clothes I wore," he said, "or maybe it was the way I talked. Everywhere I went people seemed to take an instant dislike to me. But I've finally put it together."

Anne shrugged. "I should have told you right at the start, but somehow I couldn't find a way of accusing you of being a spy without hurting your feelings."

"A spy!" He was startled.

She nodded. It was time to be totally honest. "People around here think you came to town while my dad was away to look into how he was running the store. You have a right to do that, of course, but it was the fact that you waited until he was gone."

Their hot chocolate was deposited unceremoniously in front of them, so Jay had to wait to reply.

To Anne's surprise, he laughed. "My dad sent me here because he said Dave Hollis was the best manager in the chain and he wanted me to get a look at how a really good store is operated."

It was Anne's turn to be surprised. "He thinks Dad's a good manager?"

"Sure. And I told you already how he keeps talking about my getting my master's in business administration and then going to work for the chain. He said managing a store the way Dave Hollis does it isn't dull, that he makes it part of the whole community."

Anne covered her face with one hand. "And we thought . . ." She couldn't finish, but picked up her hot chocolate and sipped it, barely tasting the creamy liquid.

She didn't like to talk about what they'd thought. It was too embarrassing. Instead, she hurriedly drank her chocolate.

"Let's go over to the store," she said. "Mom and Dad are going to be there and we can tell them all about everything."

" If you think it's a good idea," he answered dubiously.

Earnestly Anne leaned toward him. "Someone's going to tell them before the day is over. And I want them to get the straight story, not the rumors and lies. I want them to like you."

"Then let's go." Jay put his half-finished cup of chocolate down. Anne was conscious of Mr. Ryerson's frowning look following them as they left the drugstore.

Jay parked the red Corvette in Ogden's parking lot and they walked toward the front of the store. It was Sunday and the store was closed, but Anne could see her mother inside, moving along the aisles, straightening and examining.

She tapped on the glass door, and when her mother looked up, she motioned to her to let them in. But instead, both of Anne's parents came to the door.

"We just finished checking things over," Mom said. "And I bought some pajamas for the girls." It was obvious that she was trying not to look curiously at her daughter's new friend, but Anne could see sparks of interest in the eyes of both her parents.

"This is Jay Ogden," she said.

"Hello, Mr. and Mrs. Hollis." Jay shook hands formally, something of his old reserve in his manner.

To Anne's surprise her parents didn't comment on his name, didn't even glance up at the huge Ogden's sign above the store building. It was as if they didn't even notice the connection.

"We've been out at the hospital visiting your sisters,"

Dad told Anne. "They're both well enough to be eager to get home again."

"Dr. Gardiner says they can go home tomorrow," Mom added.

"That's good. We'll go up to see them later." She looked questioningly at Jay.

"Sure." He nodded.

Dad glanced at his watch. "We're getting a slow start on this day. We've missed morning church services entirely, but we might as well make the rest of Sunday a normal day by lunching out. How about the two of you joining us?"

"We nearly always eat out after church," Anne explained. "Sometimes we drive out to the restaurant near the old fort."

"We could do that," Dad agreed, "or we might elbow some of the high-school crowd out of the way and order some of Mr. Ryerson's homemade chili."

"It's the first time it's been cold enough for Mr. Ryerson's chili since last winter," Anne said decisively as an idea began to form in her mind.

"It's not that cold today." Mom sounded surprised.

"I'm still trying to warm up after yesterday," Anne explained.

Dad laughed. "Chili it is."

Instead of driving, they left the cars at Ogden's and walked back to Ryerson's, chatting as they strolled. At the soda fountain, the size of the crowd had increased. Anne's mother looked somewhat nervously at the hoards of teenagers, but then grinned.

"Next Sunday you have to go to the fort restaurant with us," she whispered to her daughter.

"It's a deal," Anne whispered back.

Normally it would have been embarrassing to be seen at the teen hangout with her own parents, but she had chosen to go to Ryerson's for a reason. Let all the busybodies see for themselves that Mom and Dad accepted Jay's presence!

"How about we take that booth in the back, John?" Dave Hollis asked Mr. Ryerson.

Mr. Ryerson stared unhappily at the little group. "Hope your girls are doing okay, Dave."

"Fine." Dad nodded. "Going home tomorrow."

"That's good." Mr. Ryerson's face was red and he looked about ready to burst. He stared at them for a moment longer, his gaze concentrated on Jay. "I don't know about everybody else, Dave," he finally said, "but I've got to say my piece."

Dave Hollis looked mildly surprised. "What's the matter, John? Did you buy something unsatisfactory at Ogden's?"

"I'd tell you if I did." Ryerson was speaking in a loud voice and the crowded booths and even the stools around the fountain itself were suddenly silent. Conversation had stopped and everyone was listening.

Anne felt like a spectator. She saw her parents, looking polite and puzzled. Jay seemed braced for what they both knew was about to happen.

If she'd only gotten a chance to talk to Mom and Dad first, to tell them about it, she thought belatedly.

Even a burly, middle-aged stranger who'd just walked in the front door seemed attracted to the scene, his eyes riveted to the little group in front of the fountain.

"Spit it out then, John," Dave Hollis ordered genially. He still seemed to think it was some kind of joke, but Mr. Ryerson was hopping mad.

"I'd think someone would have the common decency to tell you what's been going on behind your back. At least your own daughter could tell you!"

Anne tried not to squirm. Mr. Ryerson was so hard-headed. Even when he was told the whole truth, he'd probably still be hard to convince.

"Mr. Ryerson, you don't understand," she tried to explain.

He ignored her. "Do you know who this boy is, Dave?" he queried sharply, jabbing a long finger right up against Jay's chest. Anne stepped protectively closer to her friend.

"Just listen, Mr. Ryerson," she tried again to talk.

He was too caught up in his own indignation to listen.

"This boy!" He jabbed at Jay again. "This boy is a snake in the grass, Dave."

Dave Hollis looked uncomfortable. "Now really, John, you're talking about Anne's friend. I'm sure—"

Mr. Ryerson wasn't letting anybody finish a sentence. "You don't know a thing about it, Dave. But your boss sent this boy down here to snoop around your store while you were gone. And the thing that gets me is that your own daughter aided and assisted him."

"You can't blame Anne!"

Anne stared in total shock as Mrs. Turner stepped from behind a cosmetics display on the opposite side of the store, striding toward them so indignantly that even the elaborate blond upsweep of her hair seemed to quiver. She still had a packaged tube of lipstick in her hand and she shook it vehemently at Mr. Ryerson. "She's only a child and she didn't know what she was doing." Her gaze skidded past Anne to focus on Jay. "Young man, I know your father owns the chain, and goodness knows I need my job, but there comes a time when a person has to stand up and be counted. Dave Hollis is a fine manager, Sue Hollis is the best bookkeeper we've ever had, and Anne . . ." She hesitated, glancing doubtfully at Anne. She had to struggle with herself before speaking further. "With my training, Anne may be a fine manager herself one of these days."

In spite of the uncomfortable moment, Anne could barely keep from smiling. A real compliment from Mrs. Turner!

"But, you, young man, to come down here and take advantage of Anne's good nature to displace her father from his job!"

"You might as well face facts, young fellow," Mr. Ryerson said with a glower. "And get back where you're wanted. You're not needed here."

Anne had almost forgotten the presence of others here, but she heard a murmur of approval from the high-school crowd. Obviously these were juniors and seniors . . . and perhaps a few freshmen. Sophomores would have better taste.

She felt her own anger rise, but before she could come

to Jay's defense, the stranger she'd noticed earlier stormed into their midst.

"Dad!" She heard Jay's voice.

But the thickset man was looking at her father, shaking his fist in his face. "Now you've spoiled everything, Dave Hollis! I sent my boy to you because I thought you'd help get him involved in the business and instead you've got a whole town full of people mistreating him."

"Now, Harry," Dad said soothingly. "Hold on a minute."

"Yeah, Dad. Take it easy." Jay tried to put his hand on his father's shoulder, but the man shook it off without noticing.

"I don't need people like you working for my company," he informed Dave Hollis.

Dave and Leslie were alike, both slow to anger, but when they got mad, look out! Anne watched the color rise in her father's face.

His tone was icily polite. "Then perhaps it's best that I resign."

"If that's what you want." Harry Ogden returned the words like a tennis player slapping a ball back across the net. "Personally I'd prefer to have the pleasure of firing you." He turned to go. "Come on, Jay. We're getting out of this town." He stalked toward the door, pushed it forcefully open.

Jay looked helplessly at Anne. "I've got to go after him. Getting mad like that isn't good for his heart. I've got to make sure he's all right."

Anne nodded, then watched as he ran after his father. She turned back to her own parents.

Mom looked dazed. "Dave, you can't mean it. You're going to leave Ogden's after all these years?"

Dad's mouth was set in a stubborn line. "I won't change my mind," he said. "We might as well start packing."

11

It seemed to Anne that next morning that she was the only member of the Hollis family going on with life in the usual way. Normally, even though Mom and Dad had returned early from vacation, they would still have gone down to check on things at the store. But this morning, neither of them had even set foot out of the house.

Leslie and Nikki were still in the hospital and Mom would be bringing them home later in the day. Dad was already calling contacts within the retail industry, seeking information about job opportunities.

Instead of bustling about with her usual morning routine before reporting for duty in the store, Mom sat at the kitchen table, sighing over a cup of coffee.

It was still twenty minutes to eight, time for a slice of toast and some juice. Anne wasn't hungry, but she needed to talk to her mother.

She put bread in the toaster, then slumped into the chair next to Mom.

"Are we really going to move?" she asked. "Even now that you know about Jay and his reason for being here?"

Mom stared out the back window behind the dining area. Leaves fluttered from frostbitten trees. "I'll never like another place as well as Bryan," she said. "Before your dad and I moved here, we lived in one suburb after another and they all looked so much alike I can't even keep them straight in my memory."

Bryan had never before seemed special to Anne, but now that she was about to leave it . . .

"I may not see Jay again. His father probably has dragged him back to Houston already."

"I don't think so." Her mother assumed a thoughtful

130

air. "Harry Ogden called last night to talk to your father. But Dave wouldn't speak to him."

"What do you suppose he wanted?"

Mom shook her head. "I've no idea. You've got to understand, Anne, that your father is hurt."

Anne frowned. "He knows neither Jay nor I wanted to harm him."

"He's been a valued employee of Ogden's for so many years, and to have Harry Ogden turn on him and say such things, totally without justification." Mom's voice shook with sudden anger. "Dad has certainly earned Mr. Ogden's trust."

Anne started to argue, but then realized she knew exactly what her mother meant. It was the way she'd felt when Jay didn't believe her, when he thought she was only being nice to him because of her dad's job.

They'd never entirely cleared that up. Maybe they'd never have the chance now.

She wasn't hungry. She wouldn't even be able to choke down the toast. She left it still in the toaster and started for school.

It wasn't the first time a red Corvette had been parked in front of her house; she didn't know why she was surprised to see it.

Without hesitation, she walked to it and got in beside Jay. "Hi," she said.

"Got a minute to talk to me before school?"

"I'll even be late if I have to."

"Maybe we'd better drive around. Someone might come out of the house any minute now."

"Mom's still wearing her bathrobe, so I don't think she's going anyplace for a while. And Dad . . . well, he's upstairs making phone calls."

"I'm sorry about yesterday, Anne. My dad blows up too easily these days. I think it comes from being sick, but I had to get him out of there and get him calmed down."

"Is he calm now?" Anne asked dubiously. It was hard for her to imagine even-tempered Jay with such an explosive parent.

Jay shrugged. "He's not telling, but he's not talking it

over with me either. He says we're leaving town as soon
as he can get things organized at the store. He won't even
listen to me when I try to tell him what really happened
yesterday."

Anne nodded glumly. "Mom and Dad listened, but
they say it doesn't make any difference. Dad feels insulted
and he's already looking for another job."

"They won't listen to us," Jay agreed. "We're their own
kids. Now, if we could get someone else to talk to them,
they'd have to be polite enough to listen."

"But there isn't anyone to do it," Anne said. Then she
straightened abruptly, giving a little laugh. "I know who
can do it!"

"What do you have in mind?"

"I could talk to your dad and you could talk to my
parents," she suggested eagerly. "Maybe we'd have better
luck convincing each other's family."

Jay's expression said he didn't think it could be that
simple. He looked doubtfully toward her house. "Your
mom and dad barely know me."

Anne grabbed his hand. "Give it a try," she pleaded.
"Otherwise it's back to Houston for you and who knows
where for me. We may never see each other again."

He grasped her hand. "We'll find each other," he exclaimed, his voice rough with feeling. "I love you, Anne."

Anne caught her breath. It had been one thing that
night at the hayride to talk about love at first sight. That
was playing at love. But the sound of Jay's voice told her
this was different.

She tried to analyze her own feelings. It wasn't easy.
All she knew was that she cared more for him than for
any other boy she'd ever known.

She rested her face against his shoulder. "Are we going
to do it, then?" She avoided the subject of love. "You'll
talk to Mom and Dad?"

"You could convince me of almost anything," he told
her softly.

She pulled away. "When would be a good time for me
to talk to your dad?"

"He'll be working at the store all day."

"When I go to work I'll look for him," she decided.

"What about me? When should I try to talk to your parents?"

Anne looked at the big two-story house. Its windows glittered like closed eyes in the early-morning light, except for two spots—her parents' upstairs bedroom, where Dad was making his calls, and the kitchen, where Mom sat trying to figure things out.

"How about right now?"

"Now?" He sounded totally terrified.

She grinned. "They won't bite you. Just march up the walk, ring the bell, and when Mom answers the door, ask to talk to them."

He looked at her, looked at the house, then back at her again. "It might be a good idea to get it over with so I don't have to dread it all day. But a kiss would give me extra confidence."

She raised her eyebrows. "You really think that would help?"

"Definitely," he assured her solemnly.

They were laughing so hard that the kiss was hardly romantic, and when they pulled away from each other, Jay looked past her in horror.

"Someone just looked out," he said. "I think it was your mother."

"Oops!" Anne grinned at him. "Now you do have your work cut out for you. You've got to convince Mom and Dad not only of your father's good intentions, but of your own."

"Mr. and Mrs. Hollis," he mumbled, obviously practicing his speech, "you could not have seen me kissing Anne out front, and if you did, it must have been a figment of your imaginations."

"Lying will get you nowhere," Anne told him. They got out of the car and Anne started down the walk toward school while Jay proceeded slowly toward the front door. "Good luck," she called.

"You too," he returned.

Anne didn't get too much out of school that day. She kept finding herself rehearsing her own little talk.

She understood now what Jay had meant by saying that

by talking to her parents first thing, at least he wouldn't have to dread it all day.

By the time school was over, the dread had ballooned in her stomach. She hurried toward the store, wishing she could turn and walk in another direction.

The store was crowded with customers when she arrived and Mrs. Turner had more than she could do trying to help several people at once. Anne didn't have a chance to do anything but work so hard she wouldn't even think about Mr. Ogden. But by five the crowds had melted away and the department was empty.

"Mrs. Turner," she said, "is Mr. Ogden still in the store?"

Mrs. Turner gestured toward the elevated office on one side of the store. "He's been up there all day. I've felt like he was watching each move I've made."

"I need to talk to him. Would it be all right if I took off for a few minutes?"

"I can't believe this. Ogden's without the Hollis family isn't to be imagined." She sounded close to tears, but Anne was less surprised than she'd expected. She had learned that there was more to Mrs. Turner than what showed on the surface.

"Is it all right if I take the time off, then?" she asked.

Mrs. Turner nodded. "Go ahead," she said, sniffing. She turned away without another word, folding clothes in a disarranged display as though embarrassed to be caught with her feelings so visibly displayed.

Anne went around to the storage area of the store and climbed the familiar stairs to her father's office. Well, it used to be his office.

At the door, she tapped cautiously.

"Come in," a voice barked at her.

She stepped inside. The little office was above the store, like a balcony, and from this position the manager could observe the entire floor below. But also like a balcony, the side walls came only to about her waist, so raised voices could be heard on the floor below. Anne knew she could keep her voice low, but after the meeting with Mr. Ogden, she doubted if he knew how to speak softly.

He was busy at the desk and it was a moment before

he swung his chair around to look at her. He glared fiercely.

Now she could see some resemblance to Jay. Already the boy was taller than his father, and Harry Ogden was heavily built in contrast to his slim son. But the thinning hair was sandy red and his green eyes were like an older version of Jay's.

But there was no sparkle of gentle humor in those green eyes. "What have you been doing to my son?" he asked.

At least there was no need to introduce herself. Obviously he knew who she was.

"Jay and I have become good friends," she answered cautiously.

"Good friends! You're fifteen and he's sixteen and he thinks he's in love with you. Refuses to leave Bryan because of you."

Anne blushed furiously. She'd no idea Jay had been so open with his father. But this was no time to debate her influence over Jay. "He won't insist on staying here once he knows I'm moving away."

His eyes narrowed as he took in her meaning. "You don't mean Dave Hollis is serious about this quitting business?"

Anne stepped forward angrily. "Serious? The way I heard it you fired him!"

He shook his head, leaning back in the unstable chair. "Would I be foolish enough to fire the best store manager in the Southwest?"

Anne stared at him in disbelief. "I was in the drugstore yesterday when you and Dad clashed," she reminded him. She was caught up in a feeling of unreality. This couldn't be happening.

"My son tells me I misunderstood the situation, that you and your sisters were his only friends against the rest of the town."

Apparently Jay had been wrong about his dad not listening to him. She shook her head trying to clear it.

Ogden pointed to a nearby chair. "Sit down, Anne, and let's have a little talk."

Anne did as directed.

"The way I see it, the reaction of the town was just another example of how Dave's a good manager. In the years he's been here he's made himself a part of the community and that's the way it should be."

"We've lived here since my oldest sister was a baby," Anne pointed out. "And she's nineteen. We should be part of things by now."

"And it would never do to make a change. Anne, you've got to convince your dad to stay. Surely he can understand my getting a little upset when I thought my son was threatened."

Anne grinned. "A little upset!"

He grinned back and now the sparkle was in his eyes too. "My son says I have a hot temper." His face sobered. "My doctors tell me I've got to learn to control it."

Anne had a feeling that his temper was about the only thing Harry Ogden didn't control. He was certainly used to taking charge of other people. Though she instinctively liked him, she knew he was using her to hold on to her father as manager.

"I'll talk to Dad," she promised, "but I don't know how he'll feel about staying." She got to her feet.

"Do your best." He waited until she had a hand on the doorknob before speaking again. "About Jay."

She turned to look at him again.

"He likes this town in spite of everything that's happened here. He'd like to stay and go to school in Bryan. And since my forced retirement, I've been looking for a place for the two of us to settle down."

Anne's heart beat faster. If Dad could be persuaded, if Jay could remain in Bryan . . .

Too many ifs. What was the catch? She was sure the wily Mr. Ogden had one in store for her.

"The Ogden's chain has been my life," he confided. "And I'd like to see my son take over for me once he gets through college. But he won't listen to me. You know how it is, Anne. Kids never listen to their own parents."

Anne was reminded of her conversation with Jay that very morning about how parents didn't listen to their children. Maybe a lot more was coming through than either side realized. "Jay knows you want him to be a part of Ogden's. He's talked to me about it several times."

"But he refuses."

Anne shrugged. "He does have a mind of his own. You might even say he can be stubborn."

Harry Ogden smiled. "Are you trying to tell me that is a hereditary weakness in my family?"

"Oh, no, I would never say such a thing," she assured him politely.

Their eyes met and Anne knew they understood each other perfectly.

Ogden cleared his throat noisily. "The thing is that my son seems to think he can't live without you."

Anne was troubled by what he said. "I care a lot about Jay," she tried to explain, but it was difficult because she hadn't gotten a chance to sort out her own feelings yet. The only thing to do was take refuge behind the excuse of her age. "But I'm only fifteen."

He nodded and she knew he was not really listening. "I've told him we'll stay here if he'll begin to take part in the business the way you do, Anne. He can go to college here in town, and when he's through, he'll be ready to take an active part in the chain."

Anne stared in openmouthed surprise. "You mean he can stay in Bryan if he promises to plan a career in your business?"

He nodded. "That's the deal. And it's up to you to convince him to stay, Anne. I'm sure you can do it."

"I don't know if it would be right for him."

"You do want him to stay, Anne?" he asked.

Slowly Anne nodded. "Yes," she whispered. "I want Jay to stay."

Without another word, she left the office and started down the stairs.

"You can do it, Anne," he called after her.

It was nearly time to go off duty by the time she got back to her department. She offered to stay overtime, but Mrs. Turner shook her head. "Doesn't look like it's going to be a busy evening," she said.

Even though they hadn't made an arrangement to meet, Anne hoped to see the Corvette waiting outside the store, but it wasn't there. Instead, her mother sat in the family clunker.

Exhausted, Anne climbed into the front seat. "How are we going to get our car back from California?" she asked.

"Your father's making arrangements," Mom commented vaguely, then grimaced. "He's been making all sorts of arrangements today. He's already gotten a job offer, a very good one."

Anne's heart sank. "Where?"

"It's near Chicago."

"I guess that would be a nice place to live." Anne tried to sound positive, but it was hard. Right now there was no place other than Bryan where she really wanted to live.

"Did Jay talk to you?" She tried to sound casual.

Mom nodded. "What he said made a lot of sense. I can accept the circumstances as explanation for his father's behavior, but I'm not even sure Dave was listening."

Mom sounded as unhappy about the possibility of a move as Anne felt. "Maybe he'll cool off and think it over," she suggested.

"Maybe." Mom didn't sound hopeful. "Leslie and Nikki are home," she said, sounding suddenly like her usual cheerful self. "And we're having a special dinner. Your father splurged on steaks and he's grilling them himself."

"Oh, good," Anne tried to sound enthusiastic. Somehow she wasn't particularly hungry tonight.

Mom parked the car in the driveway next to a red Corvette.

"I invited a guest for dinner," Mom said.

Anne didn't have to ask who the guest was.

Inside, she found Leslie stretched out on the living-room sofa and Nikki sitting in the big chair, an enormous cast dwarfing her small body. They were in the middle of a hot debate, but Anne wasn't even interested in finding out what they were arguing about. It was just good to have everybody back home.

Leslie glanced up at her. "Your friend is out back helping Dad," she said.

Anne started to go look for Jay, but he and Dad came

in just then. Dad was carrying the long fork he used when charcoaling steaks.

"I've been teaching this young man the secret of cooking a juicy, perfect steak," he explained, bending to give Mom a kiss.

Jay looked searchingly at Anne. "How did it go?"

Anne glanced at her parents.

"They know about our plan," Jay said. "I told them."

Dad settled on the arm of Nikki's chair. "Not that it matters, but how did Harry react?"

"He said you were the best manager around and he couldn't afford to lose you. He said he was sure you'd understand why he got upset and misunderstood what was going on."

Anne thought she detected a pleased expression on her father's face, but it was quickly banished. "I've already got a good offer. I have to give it serious consideration."

Anne studied her father's face while Jay and the rest of the family remained silent. Then she grinned. "You're not really going to leave, Dad," she accused. "You want Mr. Ogden to have to beg and plead a little to convince you to stay."

Dad got to his feet. "That's not it," he grumbled. "But I've got to consider the best interests of my family. Everyone must help decide."

"I'll be much too unwell to travel for ages yet," Leslie said in a weak voice from her place on the sofa.

"I'm already enrolled in college here, Dad. Even if the rest of you leave, I'll still have to plan on staying." Nikki sounded troubled.

"I don't want to leave." It was Mom's turn. "Anyway, I didn't resign *my* job."

Dad didn't look terribly disturbed at this opposition. He turned to Anne. "What about you?" he asked. "You going to join the rest and mutiny on me?"

Anne didn't answer. Instead, she looked at Jay. "Will you be going away?"

"Dad says we are." His jaw was set in a stubborn line and she was reminded of what his father said about his refusing to leave Bryan.

She turned back to her father. "Two days ago I wanted

to leave Bryan more than anything. I thought everybody here was hateful and awful." She paused to smile at a memory. "But when Mrs. Turner spoke up for me yesterday at Ryerson's, I realized that even when people are bossy and difficult . . . well, it's because they care. We're a part of things here, Dad."

Her father's amused look vanished. "That's very perceptive of you, baby."

"I don't understand," Leslie spoke up. "If I was Anne, I'd be furious with the way everyone pokes their noses into her business. I mean, everyone's been absolutely terrible to Jay too. I don't see why he wants to stay."

At Leslie's words, the others looked at Anne. She knew they were thinking it was only because of her that he wanted to stay.

"Your dad's anxious for you to get involved in the chain," she told Jay. Somehow she was reluctant to tell him about the exact conversation. He would be very angry if he knew his father had asked her to influence his decision.

Jay nodded. "He's mentioned that."

She knew that was an understatement. From Mr. Ogden's conversation, she suspected he talked to Jay about little else these days. Somebody should tell him that was the last way to get his son interested.

But then nobody needed to tell him. He'd thought of a new way: through Anne.

"Those steaks should be about ready," Dad told them. "Do you two sickies want to be served in here or can you join the rest of us in the dining room?"

"I can manage," Leslie answered, adding quickly, "but I'm not up to doing dishes."

"You're really making the most of this," Nikki accused, swinging to her feet and reaching for her crutches. "Poor Anne will be left doing chores for both of us. And after she carried the whole load the day we were hurt."

Dad stopped and turned to look at Anne. "Dr. Gardiner and Mrs. Madison have both been singing your praises," he told Anne. "I'm proud of the maturity you showed in the emergency."

"Guess we can quit worrying about Anne." Nikki

spoke softly, but with a note of surprise. "She's grown up a lot lately."

"Maybe she's been grown up for quite a while and we just hadn't noticed," Mom added.

Everything was getting too serious. "Then you'll quit referring to me as the baby of the family?" she asked with a grin.

"Never!" Leslie said.

"Not for a long time, anyway." Nikki shook her head.

Anne and Jay waited until the others had gone into the dining room, lingering behind for a moment alone.

"Looks like everything's beginning to work out," he said, hugging her quickly against his side.

Anne couldn't answer. She couldn't feel very optimistic. If she didn't persuade him to do as his father wanted, he would be leaving very soon.

She had to do it. She couldn't bear to have him leave.

12

After dinner, Anne and Jay got into his car and drove in the fading light of the evening toward the mountains.

"This is the first chance in ages we've had to be alone," Jay told her.

Anne nodded, conscious that this was her chance to convince Jay that his father was right and he should choose a career with the Ogden chain. It was the only way she could keep from losing him.

Instead, she admired the evening through the car window. Stars sparkled so brightly they seemed almost to sit on top of the low mountains. She sighed.

He spoke before she could. "I believe your dad will choose to stay with Ogden's, don't you?"

Anne nodded. "He loves Ogden's," she agreed.

"And I love you." It was a matter-of-fact statement, simple as saying the moon was in the sky, but it rocked her.

He'd said once she could talk him into anything. Now she had to talk him into a career at Ogden's.

"I like working there too," she said by way of introduction.

"You're the one who should plan on going into management," he told her. "You have a talent for it."

This wasn't working out the way she'd planned. She'd have to be more subtle. "What do you plan to do when you're older?" she asked.

He drove in silence, moving cautiously along the darkening mountain roads. "I don't know. I might even be interested in the stores someday. But, Anne, it's too soon to be narrowing my choices. I want the whole world to choose from. I don't even know what I'll be like when I'm twenty-five, and managing Ogden's may be the furthest thing from what I'll want."

Anne didn't answer. A crushing weight had settled on her chest. Nikki had bragged about how grown-up her little sister was getting to be. Maybe being grown-up meant having to recognize when you had to let the people you cared for make their own choices.

"Remember this place?" Jay asked suddenly. He turned the car off the road.

She grinned. "I should. I brought you here in the first place." It was the turnoff where they'd once viewed Bryan together. It was the place where he'd first kissed her.

They got out together, pulling their coats more closely against the chilly night air. Anne couldn't help feeling a little sad. It was almost as if it was already over, and she was looking back on the times when she'd come here with Jay.

They leaned over to look far down below at the town, brightly lighted in the autumn night.

"A girl once told me she could identify her house from way up here," he said.

"It's that light right over there," Anne assured him, pointing.

He grabbed her outstretched hand and used it to pull her to him. He kissed her, then held her back away from him so he could see her face. "I'm not going to leave. I'll do whatever I have to so that I can stay with you."

Anne was troubled by the seriousness in his tone. "I'd like to see you stay, but don't make any permanent agreements because of me. You might be in love with Susan Michaels in six months' time and you'd be stuck with the deal you'd made."

"Susan Michaels!" He sounded shocked. "I told you I love you, Anne, and all you can say is that Susan Michaels will probably be next on my list?"

"She's a pretty girl." Anne felt contrary. "You've got to realize we're still young, Jay. We'll probably fall in and out of love a dozen times before we finally settle down to the real thing."

He sat down abruptly on the edge of a boulder, staring reproachfully up at her. "How can you talk like this?"

Anne shrugged. "It's what everyone says. Puppy love and all that!"

"It's not like that!"

Anne wanted to agree. She wanted to tell him she loved him as much as was possible. But she couldn't. She couldn't let him agree to his father's plan because of her.

"You're the first boy I ever really dated. I don't have anything to compare things with. Anyway, you'll be going away soon. Surely you don't expect me to sit around the house waiting until we're out of high school, or maybe even college, and can see each other again?"

"Well, no, but . . ."

Anne swung down the path toward the car. She had to get this over with fast before she buckled under the pressure. She felt like crying, but she kept her voice light. "We'll write, but not too often. I want you to give yourself a chance to get to know other girls and I plan to be like Leslie and have so many boyfriends I can hardly count them."

He grasped her so suddenly that she lost her breath.

He held her tightly, staring into her face. "You're not Leslie. You're Anne, and you're playing some kind of game with me and I don't understand why. You're scaring me by acting this way. It's as though I don't have anyone left to count on."

She found him hard to resist. Her mouth was so dry she couldn't speak.

When she did manage to speak again, all pretense was gone. "I don't want you to go away, Jay, but neither of us has much choice. And if that's what must happen, then I really do want you to give yourself a chance to like other girls."

His grip on her arms relaxed. "And the way we feel about each other? It isn't just one of a dozen romances?"

She was forced to smile up at him. "It doesn't feel that way. But, Jay, we've found each other so early. We've got a long way before we can be sure of anything. It's like you said about working for your dad, neither of us knows what kind of person we'll be at twenty-five."

"But I love you, Anne." His voice was desperate again.

"And I love you . . . for now. But I can't get all serious and make promises for the future. Life's still a whole exciting adventure ahead of us."

He still looked reluctant. She pulled loose from his arms. "Jay, I know how it is. You don't have a mom and your dad is sick. You want someone solid in your life. That'll come in time. Maybe it'll even be me."

He managed to laugh. "How come you're so smart?" he teased gently, leading the way to the car.

"I'm smart about you because I care," she confessed.

They got in the car and started the drive back to Bryan.

"I'd like you to stay," she told him, "but even if it isn't possible, you can visit. Perhaps your dad will send you out to see how the Ogden's manager is doing."

"I've still not given up on living here. I like Bryan, or think I could like it if I'm given a chance. I want to try and make a place for myself in a town like this, where people really get to know one another."

"Maybe your dad will find a town about the size of Bryan," Anne suggested, trying to pave the way for the disappointment he was bound to feel when he realized his father wasn't going to give in.

He frowned at her. "You talk as though you already know I won't be staying."

Anne thought quickly. She'd gotten into trouble with him before because she hadn't told the whole truth. "When I talked to your father this afternoon, he as much as said so."

He kept his eyes on the road ahead. "He told you we would be definitely leaving Bryan?"

"Not exactly."

"What did he say, then?"

Anne stared out the window, counting stars to steady her mind. She had to tell him in exactly the right way to keep him from getting mad at his father.

"He talked about how much the Ogden's chain means to him, said it was his whole life, and that he wanted you to—to—"

"To follow in his footsteps," Jay finished grimly. "I've certainly heard enough about that subject."

Anne nodded. "And he said you wanted to stay here because of me and he thought it would be a good idea because you could work for my dad and learn about the store and eventually study at the college here in town," she paused, running out of words. She hoped she was explaining it right.

"He asked you to try and keep me here?" His voice was deceptively gentle. She could hear the tension underneath.

"It's only because he cares so much." She was surprised to find herself defending Harry Ogden. "He's sick, Jay, and he wants his life to count for something."

"He wants to tell everybody what to do! If he takes care of himself he'll live for years, and I intend to see that he does what the doctors say."

They were coming into Bryan now. Anne was surprised when Jay, instead of turning onto the street that led to her house, went in the opposite direction. He went past Ryerson's and past Ogden's.

"Where are we going?"

"Dad's over at the rooming house," he explained. "We're going to talk this out with him."

"Not me!" Anne exclaimed in dismay. The last thing she wanted was to be caught between stubborn Harry Ogden and his strong-minded son.

"He wanted you to talk me into staying?" Jay asked, his voice angry.

"Well, yes," Anne admitted.

"Why didn't you do it? Don't you want me to stay?"

They stopped in front of Mrs. Fumble's rooming house. Anne looked doubtfully at the lighted windows. "I wanted you to stay," she said. "But I couldn't talk you into a career you might hate just because of something I wanted."

She didn't move when he got out of the car. Maybe he would go in the house without her.

He opened the door on her side and waited for her to get out.

"Why do I have to be a part of this?"

"Because you *are* a part of it." His answer was simple.

"And Dad's got to know how we both stand. I don't want him using us against each other."

It made sense. Reluctantly Anne walked toward the house with him.

Mrs. Fumble was on the sofa in the the front room, knitting away at an already huge afghan. She looked surprised at the sight of Anne.

"Anne Hollis, I don't believe your parents would approve of your presence here," she scolded.

Anne smiled nervously at the gray-haired woman. But Jay spoke before she could say a word. "Anne and I need to talk to my dad, Mrs. Fumble. Is he still upstairs?"

Mrs. Fumble shook her head, still looking displeased. "He's in the rec room watching television with my other guests," she said. "The news is on. That means it's getting late for a young woman who has school tomorrow."

"Wait here, Anne," Jay instructed. "I'll get my dad."

Anne sat down on the end of the sofa as far from Mrs. Fumble as she could.

"How are your sisters?" Mrs. Fumble asked.

"They're home from the hospital," Anne reported.

"I'd heard that. They say Nikki is doing very well on her crutches, but that Leslie still looks a little pale."

Anne was past being surprised when townspeople knew more about her family than she did.

"I understand young Jay is getting to be well thought of around town, now that people know he came to your father's defense," Mrs. Fumble continued. "Of course, I've been telling everyone all along that he's a fine young man." She glared at Anne as though defying her to disagree. "Any number of girls in this town would be proud to be seen in his company."

Anne couldn't help being pleased. Finally someone in this town was looking after Jay.

"He's an exceptional boy," Mrs. Fumble continued. "And that father of his wouldn't be bad if he'd slow down and live a little. I've already decided to recommend he run for school board."

"School board!" Anne was reminded of the reason for

her presence here. "But the Ogdens don't plan to live here, Mrs. Fumble."

Mrs. Fumble frowned, annoyed at this hitch in her plans. "They should. They'd be an asset to the community."

Anne was embarrassed when she looked up to find that Jay and his father had come into the room. She hoped they hadn't heard the conversation.

"It seems my son and his friend want a private conference with me, Mrs. Fumble," Mr. Ogden told her. "Is there a place where we can talk?"

"Oh, my, yes." Mrs. Fumble considered. "In here will be fine. No, one of the boarders might walk in any minute. What about the kitchen? Will it do?"

"Anyplace," Ogden assured her gruffly. Anne eyed him glumly, deciding he was already in a bad mood.

"Maybe we should talk tomorrow," she suggested.

"We're going to talk right now." Jay sounded as sure of himself as his assertive father.

The kitchen was large and old-fashioned; the equipment on which Mrs. Fumble produced her reputedly delicious meals was massively built. Anne walked over to admire half a dozen jars of strawberry preserves on the countertop.

"Mom says not many people can put up fruit like Mrs. Fumble," she commented.

Harry Ogden was listening. His eyes were on his son.

"Sit down, Anne." Jay pulled a chair out from the kitchen table, emphasizing her presence at the conference.

Ogden looked annoyed. "Seems to me this is between us, son. No need to bother Anne with our problems."

"Anne tells me you tried to make a deal with her," Jay told his father. "That if she'd talk me into going into the business, you'd choose Bryan as a retirement town."

Harry Ogden's face reddened. Anne looked down quickly, not meeting his eyes. Why did Jay have to be so blunt? Now his dad would never forgive her.

"I only want the best for you, Jay," Ogden said, sounding defensive.

"I want to stay in Bryan," Jay countered.

His father placed both hands, palms down, on the

table. "You know the agreement I offered. Begin to take part in the local store, plan on majoring in business in college, and we'll stay. It's a nice little town. I could be happy here."

Now Jay's face was red, but Anne was proud of the way he kept his temper. "No deal."

Ogden's mouth twisted wryly. "Then I guess we start packing."

It was a stalemate. Coming here had done no good. "When I was little and Mom and Dad tried to make me taste things, I was sure to hate them," Anne spoke hurriedly, hoping the thoughts she was trying to express made some kind of sense. "But when it's my idea to try something new, sometimes I like it."

Ogden frowned at her as though he'd almost forgotten her presence. "What does that have to do with—"

Jay interrupted before his father could finish. "Don't you see, Anne's trying to tell you that you're forcing the business down my throat. The only way I can ever really learn to like it is if it's my own decision. You don't want me running Ogden's some day and hating every minute of it?"

"Gosh, no!" Ogden sounded startled, as though the possibility hadn't occurred to him. "You'd run the business right into the ground."

Anne pressed the advantage. "I love working in the store, Mr. Ogden, but I had to beg my father to give me the opportunity. I do it because I want to, not because someone makes me."

Harry Ogden stared down at his own hands, sunk deep in thought. Anne and Jay looked hopefully at each other.

Suddenly Ogden looked up. "You two are trying to manipulate me." His deep voice boomed out the accusation.

Anne grinned. "Sure we are," she admitted.

He frowned a moment longer, then allowed his mouth to relax into a reluctant smile. "I like you," he said. "You're good for my son."

"Anne's a kind, thoughtful person," Jay agreed, putting his hand on hers.

"I didn't mean that." His father shook his head. "I

mean she loves Ogden's and maybe the way she feels will rub off on you."

Anne laughed and even Jay managed a faint chuckle. Harry Ogden nodded with sudden satisfaction. "We'll stay for the rest of the school year at least."

It was more than either of them had expected. Jay looked wary. "I'm not making promises," he told his father. "I'm not telling you I'm suddenly going to become fascinated with retail sales."

"I understand." His father nodded.

Jay still looked suspicious. "I'm thinking about engineering," he said, "or maybe data processing."

His father nodded again. "I suppose when that day comes I'll have no choice but to adjust. But in the meantime, I can hope." He got to his feet. "Besides, who knows, you might marry someone interested in the business. She could manage Ogden's."

He didn't even look at Anne.

"I'd better get Anne home." Jay suddenly seemed flustered, hurrying her past Mrs. Fumble with a hurried good night and out onto the porch.

Anne didn't say anything until they were in the car again. "You and your dad sure do make long-range plans for the future," she teased.

He grinned.

Back in front of Anne's house, they lingered on the front steps in spite of the cold.

"Guess I'll run over to Bryan High tomorrow and enroll," he said casually.

"I'll be looking for you," Anne told him.

"Looking for me? Can't we drive over together?"

"I suppose." She took his outstretched hand into her own. "It'll be great having you there."

"Anne, there's one thing I want you to know," he blurted out in a rush. "I know you're right about what you said about it being too soon, and there being so many years and changes ahead . . . that we can't be serious for a long time . . . and you may have a dozen boyfriends between now and then, but I just want you to know that I intend to still be around when you're twenty-five."

Anne laughed joyously. "Somehow I don't think I'll mind," she said.

"There's one more thing, Anne."

"What's that?" She frowned up at him.

He leaned close to whisper. "I'd love to kiss you good night, but Nikki and Leslie keep looking out the front window. I guess they want to know when you're coming in."

Anne laughed again. "Still the baby of the family," she said, "but I don't mind so much anymore." Then, right in full view of both her sisters, she reached up and kissed him.

About the Author

Barbara Bartholomew has sold over 100 short stories to magazines and teenage publications, including the 1980 Christmas story for *Seventeen* magazine. She lives in Dallas, Texas, with her husband and three children.